DARKEST
POWER
THE DARK ONES SAGA

PRAISE FOR THE DARK ONES SAGA

OVER 4 MILLION READS WORLDWIDE

A whirlwind of sin, sun and all things darkness and light. I adore the Dark Ones Saga.
~ Audrey Carlan, #1 *New York Times* Bestselling Author

Obsession isn't a strong enough word to describe my feelings for this series and these characters! Rachel Van Dylan has set the bar when it comes to paranormal and otherworldly creatures!
~ Patricia Rohrs, Words We Love By Blog

Vampires! Werewolves! Angels! Oh my! And just when you think this paranormal read couldn't get any better, Rachel Van Dyken interweaves them together in a beautifully written tale of two people who must face their darkest fears in order to find true love. I couldn't ask for more in a paranormal romance. Five "no fear allowed" stars!
~ *USA Today* Bestselling Author LB Simmons

I am not normally a paranormal fan, but RVD can make me like just about anything!
~ Heather, Goodreads Reviewer

Hot, funny, and will leave you wishing you could get marked by one of the immortals!
~ *New York Times* bestselling author, Molly McAdams

Mythology with a dash of paranormal and a shot of fantasy. It's the most amazing and lethal combination. My heart and emotions were feeling the effects of RVD's words. I simply couldn't get enough of the characters and this series.
~ Darlene, it.sgottabethebooks

Rachel's created a fantastic world that I adored living in, full of characters I want to hang out with. A fun, and sexy read! I can't wait for more from her Dark Ones Saga!
~ Author Nazarea Andrews

RVD is dangling a cool and unique look at the paranormal world she has given life to. The Creator is weaved throughout the tale of vampire, werewolves, gods, and Fallen. It is a very unique and wonderful place to be-Seattle. Lol.
~ Becky Rendon, Goodreads Reviewer

DARKEST POWER

THE DARK ONES SAGA

#1 *New York Times* Bestselling Author
RACHEL VAN DYKEN

Darkest Power
The Dark Ones Saga® Book 6
by Rachel Van Dyken®

Japanese quotes from www.fluentin3months.com/japanese-proverbs

DARKEST POWER
Copyright © 2022 RACHEL VAN DYKEN
ISBN: 978-1-957700-18-2

Editing by Kay Springsteen and Jill Sava
Cover & Interior Design by Jill Sava, Love Affair With Fiction

To my dad,
who kept asking for two years
when I would finish this book, who's
helped me this whole time with
research and read every page... well
I mean except the spicy ones haha.
I love you!

THE DARK ONES SAGA

EPIGRAPH

"And the god of war and sky will rise again, time holds no presence for the morning and evening star, for his eyes see all, beginning and the end. For serving the people well and overthrowing Osiris, he was brought gifts by the gods. One by one each presented him with something timeless, including an amulet made from the power of the moon. Whenever there was a full moon, the light from the sky would glow across his ancient temple, until around 385BC when the moons became less and less frequent, only appearing three times a year. People took it as a sign that Horus was displeased, so they worshipped him more and more in an attempt to temper his anger, but nothing worked. Eventually, the worship of Horus stopped. For the favored god had finally turned his back on his people—and disappeared."

Until now…

DARKEST POWER
THE DARK ONES SAGA

ONE

日野原重明

Kazoku to wa, "aru" mono de wa naku, te o kakete "hagukumu" mono desu
Family is not something that is "there," but something that is "fostered" with care and time.
~Shigeaki Hinohara, Japanese physician

Horus

Present Day Downtown Seattle, Soul Nightclub

"This is so pointless." I look around at all the moving sweaty human bodies; back and forth, the women move their hips and hold their hands over their heads, one starts to clap like she's proud of herself. Do I clap too? Even though it's painful to watch? A man approaches her and grabs her ass. I shake my head. He haWWs to know that won't go over well. "Here comes the slap."

I nearly spew out my beer when she punches him in the face, and he falls to the ground groaning. "More! More!" I cheer.

Tarek, my roommate, the bar manager, and a werewolf tosses one of the bar rags at me. "You know most people come here to dance and party, not to watch people get beat up."

I turn to him and smirk; he's wearing a black shirt that says bite me and has his shaggy brown hair pulled into one of those weird buns on his head that women seem to go crazy for. One time a girl asked if she could pull it; no idea why. "It's much like war, is it not?"

His pain-filled stare says it all, then he mutters, "You have no idea."

"Oh, I have ideas." I roll my eyes. "I've been studying the net."

"Internet."

"That's what I said." I wave my phone screen at him. "Plus, I'm on TikTok. Did you know there's an idiot who thinks he's a time traveler? As if he knows anything about the advanced concept that is time." Are all humans in this day and age dumber than when I existed? It feels like it.

Tarek grabs my phone. "Let me see—holy shit, how do you have a million followers already? You've been here a month—oh." He hands me back my phone. "That makes more sense."

"My name, Horus, god of sky? I'll just keep posting, and they'll keep worshipping."

Tarek bursts out laughing, tears form in his eyes, he holds up a hand. "Hold on, I need a minute." He laughs harder. "For a god, you're an idiot."

"You're the idiot." I stand and shove my barstool back. I don't exactly tower over him, but I am larger. Why does he always pick fights with me?

"You're posting thirst traps, dumb-dumb." He wipes the tears from his eyes. "I'm surprised you haven't been banned already!"

"Banned? Who would dare to ban me?"

"The people that don't think it's appropriate to post this." He shows me the phone. I'm facing the window with a cup of coffee, shirtless, in nothing but black boxer briefs that seem to have come halfway down my ass.

Oh yeah, I think I was in the process of getting dressed, but the sunlight hit differently, so I put my phone in one of those holder things and snapped a photo, then forgot the camera was still taking pictures.

I roll my eyes. "Nudity is normal."

"Yes." Tarek blinks slowly. "It's completely normal, but you don't just go posting for the world to see and shit man." He shows me another photo of myself. "You realize everyone who likes this next photo is because you're naked in bed with the sheets covering, like nothing but your cock, right?"

I shrug. "I was heated."

"Yup and they probably were too, looking at that pic." He laughs. "Lots of 'I'm questioning my sexuality' comments. Nice." His mocking laugh grates on my nerves. It's also extremely humbling that I'm constantly getting laughed at or mocked for not knowing how to use a toaster. Who the hell would know what one even is thousands of years ago?

Irritated, I snap, "Give that back." I grab my phone and attempt to slide it back into my too-tight black jeans pocket, giving up when I catch Tarek smirking at my struggle.

The girls have been trying to dress me lately, and I swear they buy jeans way too small; cock and ass are going to bust through one of these days. How's that my problem?

I roll my eyes and stare down at my phone. "What's the big deal about gray sweatpants anyway?"

"You're hopeless." Tarek slaps me on the shoulder. "And lucky for you, it's time for your shift, so stop attempting to get drunk and train the new hire."

My ears perk at that. I like meeting new people. I find it fascinating to watch their suffering and complaints; they're so different from the ones we used to hear during worship when people would sacrifice for favors.

Back then, they wanted good crops, they wanted success, fortune, and love. But now it seems like the only thing I hear is that people want to be famous and make a lot of money.

They don't even care about love anymore.

I toss back the rest of my beer, knowing it will sadly do nothing by the time it hits my system. I drink it because I like the taste, but getting drunk is pretty much impossible for me; it always has been.

Pity.

Maybe the girl dancing near the door would be prettier if I had those beer goggles on. She beckons me with her finger and winks. Her jet-black hair is pulled back so tight it has to hurt her head, and her lipstick is a bit smudged.

Should I save her?

I sigh. "Be right back."

"Can't save them all," Tarek calls after me.

"I can try." I speed up my pace and then stop right in front of her pressing her back against the wall.

"You're beautiful." She isn't slurring yet; that's good. "What's your name, gorgeous?"

"Horus," I say quickly. "And you? What's your pain?"

"You mean name?"

"Pain," I say again. "What's your pain?"

"I don't under—"

I tilt her chin upward toward me. "Show me your eyes."

Her lower lip trembles. "What are you doing?"

"Searching." I tilt my head to the side and press a hand to the pulse on her neck; it quickens with my touch, and then her heart finally speaks.

Lonely.

That's normal.

I pull back. "Do you like hockey?"

"Huh?"

"Hockey, the one with sticks, they play on ice and hit each other. Do you like it?" I have someone in mind for her that would be perfect, he's a bit older, but if that's not her preference, at least she'll be out and have a good time. "Do you?"

"Yeah, I actually used to go to games all the time."

For the briefest second, I detect ice in her pulse. Interesting. "Perfect, there's a game tomorrow night. Give me your name and number, and I'll have a ticket waiting for you. The person you're meeting will be wearing a red sweater and holding a pretzel. He too feels lonely but loves hockey, so you might hit it off, you might not, but I think what's important from what I can see with you is finding a connection, and you'll never find that at Soul"

Tears well in her eyes.

I lean in and press a chaste kiss to her lips. Her name is Jessica Long, age thirty-five, divorcee, no kids, she lives in the University district in an apartment she hates, and she's tired. She's a fourth-grade teacher. Wow, she just might be perfect. I pull more information through her mouth and store it away for her date. When I stop the kiss, her eyes are dazed.

"What was that?"

"That's how I say hello." I grin and hand my phone to her. "Number, Jessica?"

She frowns. "I don't think I told you my name."

"I'm good at guessing." I wave the phone in front of her. She takes it and puts her name in it.

Nodding my approval, I snatch it back. "I've got to go back to work, but maybe you should go home now? Take a nice, hot bath." My pupils dilate along with hers.

She nods slowly. "Yeah, yeah, good idea, thanks… Horus."

"Just doing my job." The one I miss.

She leaves the bar and nearly runs into another woman walking in.

This new woman… she smells different.

The newcomer has dirty blond hair pulled into a high ponytail; it's clearly been dyed, but not for a while. The dark circles under her eyes reveal extreme exhaustion. She would be flawless if she didn't look so tired, with her round innocent face and full, bow-shaped pink lips. Dark lashes slowly fan as she stares at me.

It's like just looking at me is putting her to sleep.

I shake my head and turn. "Um, sir, excuse me, I noticed the black Soul shirt on you… I'm here for my first shift and—"

Instantly, the wind is knocked out of me, something that never happens. *Well, that was unexpected.*

I hang my head and turn. "I'm your guy."

Her eyes widen.

"Training. I'm going to be training you."

"Oh!" She nods, then drops her purse onto the floor. Is she drunk? All of her things fall out, revealing an obscene amount of energy drink packets and several bottles of prescription pills.

Too bad, I'll have to fire her.

We don't allow drunks, or drug users, or girls who...

She reaches for the last bottle, then collapses right in front of me and starts to snore.

What the hell?

TWO

口は災いの元

kuchi wa wazawai no moto

"The mouth is the source of disaster."

~Japanese proverb

Kit

My eyes feel like they have sand in them, and they're so heavy that it might take someone physically peeling my eyelids back for me to be able to open them.

I hate the weekends. It's always harder for some reason, especially with the full moon, but this was the fourth job in two months that I knew would most likely fire me if I didn't show up.

I did everything right, though.

I took all my medicine on time.

I shoved caffeine down my throat.

But the minute I walked into the darkness of the club and saw him, I felt… safe, warm, and so sleepy I just… fell.

Like a drunken idiot.

I groan a bit, then something hard taps my side. "You alive?"

The voice is really deep and slightly accented, but I can't really place from where other than if the person belonging to this voice decided to start narrating audiobooks, I would be all over it.

I groan again and try to open my eyes.

His heavy and annoyed sigh isn't exactly helping the situation. It feels like I'm lying on a soft leather couch; the room smells like Bourbon and cigars.

I make another attempt to open my eyes.

Success!

It's bright above my head like I'm about to get accused of a crime and interrogated. I blink again, and a face appears in my line of vision.

I don't really have the words to explain the man I'm staring at. The club had been too dark, but now that I see the light, I don't think I ever want to turn the lights off again.

His hair is bright blond, almost white; it's wavy and kisses his broad shoulders. It's like he missed his casting call for Vikings on Netflix. His eyes are crystal blue, and he has this Henry Cavill sort of Witcher look to him that shows off his strong, flexing jaw and full lips.

I lick *my* lips in response, maybe because my body has no idea what to do other than stare, lick, stare, and hope I don't get fired.

He has a black tattoo that outlines his left eye, which reminds me of Egyptian tattoos I've seen in pictures, as the edges flick out by the corner of his eye and then trace down into an upside-down triangle. It makes his left eye look so blue it's hypnotic.

I lean forward, wanting to examine just that one eye's beauty. It's perfect, and I don't even like tattoos.

His eyes narrow. "Are you drunk?"

"No." I try to sit up and struggle to get my sluggish body in an upright position.

He doesn't help me.

I finally manage to sit straight on the brown leather couch and look around the room. It's extremely bare for an office. A few books that look older than the Bible occupy a nearly empty bookshelf. A black wooden desk with a metal chair sits in the middle of the room, but other than that, nothing.

Not even a pen.

Did he just get hired too?

I squint up at him. "How long was I out?"

"Seven hours." He crosses his arms.

"WHAT?"

"It was a joke." Then why isn't he laughing? "You were out around ten minutes and almost fell onto my boot."

Is that a cardinal sin? "Oh."

He takes a step away from me. "We drug test."

"I passed mine."

"No, you just passed out."

"I don't—" I stop myself, draw a deep breath, and start over. "Certain times, I don't sleep, so I take a lot of caffeine, and sometimes I crash. Today was one of those days. Just call me an insomniac, which is why…" My voice wavers as I try to stand on giraffe-like shaky legs. "…this is the best job for me."

"Are you Asian?" He's so blunt I'm taken back. And I kind of want to punch him for no reason. Isn't it obvious?

"Japanese American," I say, keeping my tone even. Damn, he's blunt. "My grandparents immigrated to the states back in—"

"Pretty," he interrupts me. "All right, let's get started unless you need another ten-minute nap, a cracker, or more pills from your bag?"

He's rude.

So freaking rude, I clench my teeth. I'm still unsteady on my feet. Could he have at least made sure my blood sugar was okay? Offered water? A Mountain Dew?

A peanut?

I would take a peanut.

"Yeah, let's get started," I grind out and leave my purse in his weird office.

The club music is so loud it's hard to think. Several tall tables are scattered about the club, surrounded by people laughing and drinking, taking shots, and screaming, "Shots, shots, shots."

I don't roll my eyes, though, because those very same people will be giving me tips, and I need my A-game if I want to make rent this month. With both parents dead and no family around, it seems like all I've done is struggle and attempt to sleep when I can and work when I'm not sleeping.

Yet, I never get ahead.

How nice for these folks to be able to order twelve-dollar shots on a Friday night.

I wonder what that's even like.

I'm still wondering when I slam into the giant god of a man in front of me. He hangs his head, looks over his shoulder, and then tosses his hair before tucking it behind his ears. Okay, now I'm getting Brad Pitt hair vibes.

My throat goes dry.

He seethes. "Can you not walk?"

"I walk." It's a very lame answer. I'm aware of this as his

eyes roam painfully slow, from my Adidas sneakers all the way up to my face, which I have no doubt is as pale as a piece of paper.

He shakes his head slowly. "Did you get the training manual for the drinks?"

Why do I feel like I need to salute him like he's a soldier and then bow because he's also a prince? "Yes. I memorized everything, and I have experience, so I don't think it's going to be a problem."

"You passed out minutes after walking into the bar," he just has to add. "You snored."

"I was tired."

"I've been tired for thousands of years; try me." He rolls his eyes.

"Exaggerate much?" I mumble.

"I always tell the truth," he barks back. "Now get behind the bar and make me a Dirty Thirty."

I walk around him and step behind the bar; it's a giant U-shape that has several customers already begging for drinks and a super attractive guy serving them up like he could do it blindfolded. His brown hair is pulled into a tight man bun, the swoon-worthy kind every woman wants to mess up. He has dimples, and he's super tall; not as tall as grumpy pants behind me, but still tall.

Do they only hire hot men in their thirties, or what?

I shake it off and walk over to the guy. "Hey, I'm the new trainee, and that guy behind me said to make him a drink."

The guy glances over my shoulder. "Still scowling, I see."

"Is that his thing?"

"Some might call it his kink." Hot guy winks. "But he's easily… agitated. Age does that to a person you know. I signed him up for AARP last month. He was happy about the discount until he realized what it meant. So pissed. Put all of my Jordans outside in the rain. I held a funeral, it was a whole thing."

My eyes widen. "Who does that?"

"Gods among men who look like that." He winks again. "Am I right? Oh, and I'm Tarek, by the way. Bartender by night, wolf by day."

I laugh. *What's with these guys?*

"Cute." I find myself with this weird urge to pat him on the head and curl my fingers inward to stop myself from reaching out.

Is it me?

The lack of sleep?

Or the new job?

"So, what did he want you to make?" Tarek throws a towel over his shoulder.

I have to be imagining things, but I feel like he's flirting with me to purposefully make my new trainer mad. But that would be weird; neither of them even knows me, and it's not like I stand out. I have naturally dark hair I used to dye blonde that has seen better days and pink tips at the bottom that refuse to actually take the dye and change color. I'm kind of a mess, average height, and I guess I have a nice smile. The only thing really unique about me are my light brown, almost green eyes, but people tend to be more creeped out by them than anything.

I've been told my eyes look "too deep," whatever that means.

I snap out of my musing and cross my arms nervously. "He wants a Dirty Thirty."

Tarek does a little bow toward the bar. "Give him hell."

I smile and instantly relax. I'm back where I belong, in a place where I do everything right and don't think about the nights of no sleep or the days of feeling chased by nothing but air and loneliness.

I grab one of the tall glasses and fill it with ice, then pour in a shot of Tito's, followed by a splash of lime. Cranberry juice is next, followed by some cherry juice and two dark cherries. A shot of Bacardi floats on the top with a squeeze of lime and a spicy chili-sugar agave nectar garnish.

Normally people stir the Dirty Thirty since it can be intense, but I like to think of it as a Macchiato... let the flavors settle, then you stir, but the first sip should always taste a bit strong and spicy, just like turning thirty and realizing you've done nothing with your life and only have ten years until forty, thus the name, Dirty Thirty.

The crowd intensifies, and Tarek disappears with another bartender filling orders while I bring the tall drink over to the one who never smiles.

He looks down at the drink, back up at me, then down at it. "No stir?"

I give him the same look, then shrug. "Didn't think you were so delicate. Can't you handle a bit of alcohol?"

He scoffs. "Trust me, it's not that. I'm just wondering if the first taste is going to make me gag."

I roll my eyes. "Just try it before you bring judgment." I lift the glass. "Bottoms up."

"Such a weird phrase," he grumbles, taking the glass in his massive hand. He's wearing a large gold ring on his right hand; it has the symbol of a falcon, and just above the ring is a black tattoo of an eye.

Cool, so he's part of the Illuminati.

Makes sense.

I smile at my own joke while he lifts the drink to his stupidly lush lips and takes a small sip. He doesn't cough, but I notice his eyes water a bit. They're so blue I can't tell if it's a trick of the light or if they really are starting to shed some tears.

He coughs into his hand and sets the glass down. "Again."

"What?" I grab the drink, ready to take a sip, but he snatches it away and gulps it down like he's not one more away from a hangover.

"I said"—he clears his throat—"again."

Who died and made him the expert? I may not be good at a lot of things, but I damn well know how to make good drinks.

I clench my teeth and smile. "All right, same drink?"

"Isn't that what again means?"

Where did they find this guy? Shouldn't HR be notified that the trainer has the personality of an ass?

I turn around before I say something stupid and get fired, and wedge myself between the other two bartenders. Tarek is on the far side of the bar, pouring out shots and smiling at all the girls flirting with him. One hands him a twenty that he puts in his pocket.

He makes it look way too easy.

Okay, focus.

I grab a fresh glass and repeat the process, except at the end, where I would normally add in the garnish, I decide to add some of the dark cherry juice on top with a slice of lime and orange. It will give it a similar effect. With one last sprinkle of crystalized chili powder, I make my way back to my trainer and hand the glass over. "Cheers."

He stares down at it. "This isn't a Dirty Thirty."

"You didn't like the real version of the Dirty Thirty. I assumed it was a test, so here's my version of the drink. If you hate it, I'll try again, but I figured you might like a little... twist."

His eyes flash like he's intrigued, but he abruptly looks down, grabs the glass, and tilts it back.

He starts choking immediately. The drink sloshes over the side of the glass when he sets it down on the bar top.

He wipes the back of his mouth with his arm. I'm convinced I just poisoned him, or he's allergic to limes. This is it. I've finally done it.

I guess there was one more bar owned by a similar scary guy in Chicago, Sin, was it? Though rumors have it that the bar hides some weird tiger that eats people if they get out of line and that the main guy likes to taunt the Russian mob, but there's no way that's true. At this point I wonder if I'd be safer there than staring at this giant angry God of a man. I make a mental note to contact them and wait for the inevitable words: "This isn't going to work out."

"It's good." He finally squeezes out. "Might kill a few people, but what the hell." He grabs another drink. "What made you think of altering it like this?"

"Spice," I say simply. "It's not enough to have it on the rim, where you have to lick it off, you need it in the body of the drink."

His tongue slowly rolls across his lower lip, his eyes holding my gaze. "I'm Horus, by the way."

"So I only get your name after my drinks meet your approval?"

"Yes."

"Blunt."

"Honest," he counters. "I've spent way too long wasting time on needless words and actions. You either are or aren't, so would you like to continue training now?"

I nod my head eagerly. "Yes. I would."

He starts walking away, I'm assuming I'm supposed to follow, but he suddenly stops and turns back around, drumming his fingers on the bar top. "This whole passing out thing. Is it normal for you?"

I want to lie.

Correction. I always lie. I always say no.

But today, I want to say yes. I want someone to know my struggle. Wow, how sad and pathetic is that?

All I do is work and try not to sleep.

I want to scream into the darkness of night.

And I want to cry during the day.

Instead, I force a watery smile. "I have a sleeping condition. It's bad during weird weather." True. "And when the moon is full, which sounds ridiculous even though I know it happens every time."

He nods. "It's a full moon tonight."

"Yeah." My voice cracks.

"Is it because you can't sleep or because you won't?" His eyes lock onto mine with an intensity I've never felt before like he's reading my soul and every mistake and triumph in my short forty-two-year life span.

I can't speak. He's not intimidating or even curious; I can handle those things. No, he's looking at me like he sees the pain.

He looks at me the way I look at myself.

Without hope.

THREE

知らぬが仏

shiranu ga hotoke

"Not knowing is Buddha" or "ignorance is bliss"

~Japanese proverb

Horus

I've been alive a very long time; add on the fact that I skipped ahead a few thousand years, and I still haven't seen anything like this. She has a strange feeling about her, but I know she's completely human. If she were not, I'd be able to tell right away.

I would be able to smell her essence, and while she smelled different at first, I've almost gotten used to it, and it's definitely human.

She has nothing but normal blood running through her veins, and while my powers are limited since I left my timeline and am now in modern times. It means that I'm basically half a god—at first, it was almost embarrassing that I couldn't rise the sun or set the moon, but then I realized that in this timeline, it's someone else's job.

I clearly went into retirement the minute I left Egypt with my brother Timber, also known as Anubis. It's still strange calling him by a different name from the one I'd called him for thousands of years.

But it's growing on me.

Also, it does help that our friend Alex, another immortal who happens to be a male siren, often yells out "Timber" at the most random times, usually during Timber's favorite shows, just to piss him off. He's hilariously silent during commercials though.

Last night Alex started singing a song by some musician with funny hair. I don't think I've ever seen Timber's eyes glow so gold in my entire life.

Hilarious.

I think this is the perfect timeline for him. Even if he did have to suffer for thousands of years to find his mate again, at least he's happy, at least he knows he was a demon by choice in order to claim a soul and find his again.

I shake my head and lean against the bar top. It's already last call. I can't say I hate this job; I just hate the boredom.

I want to yell at the stupid humans. Tell them who I am. That they used to worship me with awe and bring me gifts out of thankfulness that the sky still existed.

Now, I have beer stains on my shirt and just had to help clean up puke from table number nine after a girl witnessed her fiancé cheating on her when she came home early from a work trip.

I almost slip on barbecue sauce from wings that fell on the floor, but I catch my balance and look heavenward.

Is this really my life right now?

Humility. Such a thrilling experience.

I toss the bar rag onto the table and watch Kit run around and attempt to clean up all the rest of the tables in a frenzy. It's late, but I'm not tired. Gods don't really get tired; we rest out of habit. But here, I've noticed I rest a lot more. I used to be able to go days without closing my eyes, but now that I'm thousands of years in the future, taking a nap actually sounds tempting, and Mason, my other werewolf friend, said something about binge-watching Hallmark movies, whatever the hell that is, but apparently wine and socks are involved.

Truly, I question if humans have evolved or devolved. Still thinking about it.

Tarek comes up behind me. "She's pretty." He grabs the dirty rag I just threw. "I mean, if you're into mortals."

I roll my eyes. Last month he said I was going to find my mate and said to be ready. I distinctly remember flipping him off in my head, my first modern reaction in this timeline. "It's not that mortals aren't attractive. They're just stupid." I look around the club. "Should we lock up?"

"Teach her how." He points to where she was just cleaning, but she's suddenly gone. Huh! "And I'll see you upstairs?"

"Got it." I go into my office, grab the keys from the hook, and pause... Something's wrong.

I don't know what though.

Everything looks the same.

A whimper sounds from the direction of my desk.

The lights are on, but they start to flicker. I walk around to my desk and find Kit sitting underneath it, hugging her knees. "Don't fall asleep, dreams are dreams, life is life, sleep is death, awake, awake, always awake."

I would call her crazy, except her eyes are glowing yellow.

I lean down and snap my fingers in front of her.

A hand jerks out and grips my throat. She tilts her head, her smile sad. "For a god, you're really dumb."

"What are you?" I snap.

"Lost." Her lower lip trembles. "I just want to go home."

I sigh heavily. "Where do you live?"

She points to the sky with a trembling finger as a tear runs down her cheek. "Up. I need to go up!"

"Upstairs?" Did she rent the room?

She shakes her head, and her teeth start to chatter. "Don't let me fall asleep. I can't fall asleep right now."

I frown. "What happens when you do?"

Her eyes are still bright yellow. I don't understand because I know she's a human, and there isn't any glamour or spell on her at all. I would know, I would sense it, I could pull it from her, test it, taste it even.

Nothing about her ramblings or yellow eyes make sense.

Kit shakes her head over and over again. "Die. I'll die."

"You'll die if you sleep?" I clarify.

She nods her head furiously.

And I suddenly realize it's going to be a very long night for me; good thing I was just internally boasting about not needing a ton of sleep.

"Get up." I hold out my hand. She takes it. Her hands are pale and freezing. I pull her to her feet. Her eyes go back to their natural color as she slumps against me.

She's dead weight.

I slap her face lightly. "Stay awake, then."

She nods, but she's barely walking.

To save time, I pick her up and carry her back into the bar.

"Whoa." Tarek passes me on his way upstairs. "She passed out because you smiled at her or what?"

"Yes. This is the result of me smiling." I grit my teeth. "She says she'll die if she falls asleep."

"She on drugs?"

"My exact first question when she fainted in front of me a few hours ago."

Tarek leans forward, his eyes fade to black, and he sniffs her hair and then down her body. I feel weirdly possessive of the tiny human as he continues to sniff up and down her.

He jerks away. "Huh, I'm not smelling anything immortal."

"Her eyes glow yellow," I add.

He tilts his head. "And we're sure about the drugs?"

"I think we'd smell them on her, but I can always drug test her."

"Death by sleep." He nods his head slowly. "That's new."

"I know"

"Mmm." She moans in my arms. "I'm sorry, I just need to get home."

"Do you know where home is?" I ask.

She nods, then stumbles. "Could you maybe help me get there?"

It's like she's drunk, but not. I don't understand it, and I suddenly think we really should do a test on her to make sure she's okay or maybe just hospitalize her.

Tarek puts a hand on my shoulder. "I've got her address. She lives around the corner, above the deli. Just make sure she gets home safe, and we'll talk about this later."

I nod. "Right."

He eyes her up and down, then stares at me. "Interesting, isn't it?"

"What?" I frown.

"A beautiful woman can't even keep her eyes open in front of a god." He laughs. "I can't wait to tell everyone."

"Not a word."

"Word."

"Very funny."

"Have a nice walk. I'll text you her apartment number. Make sure she has her purse and keys so you can let her in."

"I'm not an idiot." I would have totally forgotten to do all of those things; it's just not normal for me to think about purses or keys or jackets, or anything that people bring with them. Why so many things? Add the whole umbrella thing since it rains or mists in the Seattle mornings, and you need a camel to pack all your things on your way to work if you don't have a car.

Tarek says nothing, but his smirk says more than words would as he waves me off and starts going upstairs.

Apparently, I need to lock up and also take the new recruit home.

I'm about ready to ask where her purse is when a tap hits my shoulder; Tarek holds out her purse and coat, salutes me, then goes back in the direction of the apartment.

Groaning, I grab her things and slowly walk her out of the bar, careful to lock up when I leave. Not that anything would really happen since Tarek would attack anyone who dared to come in after hours.

He may be sarcastic as hell and slightly annoying, but he's still a werewolf prince, powerful, and creepy with all of his predictions.

I shudder.

I hate the cold, but more than that, I hate that I actually feel cold. I've never experienced sensations of cold or hot before now, and it's even more apparent with the wet cold.

My phone goes off.

The text reads: "A1."

Kit is slumped against me while I walk her toward the corner deli; it's open twenty-four seven. The bright blue open sign flickers on and off like it's choosing different letters to use to light up each time between the letters.

She starts to snore in my arms.

I lightly tap her cheek; she startles awake and looks up at me. "Am I home yet?"

"Close." I have the sudden urge to pat down her hair and make her feel better, but it feels like weakness on my part for someone I don't even know who has already been this difficult so soon into knowing her.

The door to get into the stairs for the apartment is open already, meaning she has zero security. I bypass it and help her walk up the stairs. It smells like mold and dirt, the top stair is broken, and there are only two apartments. Hers is on the left, and it looks like someone tried to break through the wooden door.

This is where she lives? I immediately want to sit outside and make sure that she's okay, even if I am annoyed.

This is stupidity at its finest, living in a place without actual locks. I go to her door and actually push it open.

She has nothing.

Not even a bedroom.

Just a couch, one blanket, one pillow, and a small kitchen that looks like it doesn't even work.

"Thanks," she mumbles, then stumbles toward the couch and lies down. From underneath the cushion, she pulls out a random energy drink and starts chugging it. That can't be good for her. "Just gotta stay awake another three hours."

Three hours?

I sigh and walk over to her. "How are you going to stay awake?"

Her answer: "Red Bull."

I sit down on the couch. "Okay, so then what happens after the Red Bull?"

"I can finally rest." She still hasn't opened her eyes. "For at least the hours following before it repeats."

"Why?"

"You don't want to know."

"Try me." I'm irritated as it is, but none of this is making sense.

"I'm a monster," are her last words before she drinks two more Red Bulls, then turns on the TV and starts watching a show called Friends. I stay until her three hours are up, and when I get up to leave, she's already lying there, sleeping like the dead. What a weird little human.

I go to the door and look over my shoulder, the sun is pressing through the window in such a way that it makes her body glow, and toward her beautiful legs, I swear I see a white tail.

I frown.

The vision is gone in a blink.

But I could have sworn, just for a minute there, the human... was a fox.

FOUR

井の中の蛙大海を知らず

I no naka no kawazu taikai o shirazu

"A frog in the well knows nothing of the great ocean."
Those who live in a small world think that what they see is
everything; all the while, they never know about the bigger
outside world.

~Japanese proverb

Kit

I don't go to sleep until the morning. The darkness scares
me, and I know that my reality is that I have to stay awake
until sunrise. My head nods forward as light flickers in
through the window.

Something soft touches my leg; I groan and look
down. I hope to God that Horus wasn't here long enough
to see the trick of the light. Two Red Bull cans are crushed
on my table, but I have a blanket covering me. Did he do
that?

I check my phone and then get to my feet. I have maybe
one hour before I need to show up for work. It's been a while

since I've slept all day, but I know I needed it if I'm going to survive tonight.

I get up and shuffle toward the kitchen to grab more Red Bull from the fridge. It's literally one of the only things I stock up on, on a daily basis, just in case.

And it's the only thing that does the trick next to the medicine I have to take.

For some reason, the empty fridge reminds me of my empty existence. I wish I was sleeping again, dreaming about a life that could never possibly be mine. Maybe I was an author in another life? It's the only thing that would explain the bizarre dreams I always have.

Of places I've never been.

Experiences I've never had.

Lifetimes that don't exist.

I've been a princess forced into a marriage with a horribly old dictator who ended up killing me on my wedding night—write that Wattpad.

I've been blind and forced to beg on the streets before getting run over by a horse and crippled, only to have the doctor who fixed me up fall for me and ask me to marry him. In my dreams, he always takes care of me until I die five years later from pneumonia.

And my favorite one—I was an animal. All I remember in those dreams are that I'm happy, I'm running, I'm seductive, cunning, beautiful, and protective of my fur, whatever that means. A man visits me and tells me to wait that he'll always return to me. I almost always wake up with a smile on my face afterward, like I'm finally at peace.

Which is really pathetic that I'd rather be an animal that can't even communicate than a human, even in my fantasies.

Maybe I was a dog in my past life.

A cricket.

An ant.

Who knows if I even believe in past lives, but the dreams seem so real that part of me wonders how or why I'm able to construct something so real. Experts say that everyone you see in your dreams are people who you've actually seen in real life; the human brain isn't capable of creating a new face, so that means every single face I've seen in those dreams is a face I've seen in passing.

Creepy when I think about it.

I start chugging my red bull and go charge my phone. I need to change for work; otherwise, grumpy Horus is going to get even more grumpy, and I'm already going to have another long night trying not to sleep, especially since tonight I get off early, which means it will be an even longer night where I have to drink caffeine and watch TV until the sunrise.

I try not to let it ruin my mood and change into the tight black SOUL T-shirt. I put on my black tights and black jean shorts and pair them with white Converse, then look in the mirror. I'm not wearing much makeup, but when I was hired, the owner, Timber, did say that I could do whatever sort of makeup I wanted.

I haven't really done anything in a while to my eyes, so I grab some red eyeliner and pair it with some purple eyeshadow, then extend the lines past my lids onto my temples, creating a mismatched angel wing, then color it in with the purple. I line the inside of my eyelids with the red and add some blush, then glide on some bright red lipstick. After all that, I braid my hair back into two small pigtails.

"Well," I say, staring at myself in the mirror, "this is as good as it's going to get."

I lie to myself and say that I don't care what Horus's reaction will be, and I repeat that same mantra in my head the entire walk to the bar, only to open the main door to the bar, walk by his office and nearly trip over my own feet when I see him changing his shirt.

He's half-naked.

His jeans are so tight I swear his ass might burst through the seams. He's balling the white T-shirt into his hands and tossing it onto his desk, only to grab it again and toss it one more time as if the shirt pissed him off. My mouth goes dry when he leans over the desk and grips it with his hands like he needs it to steady him.

He stills.

My feet won't move.

His head crooks to the side, but he doesn't turn around. "It's rude to spy on someone."

"It's rude to change in public," I say right back before covering my mouth with my hands.

His back muscles flex; it's like watching a god in real life. How is he that ripped and tall at the same time? His bronzed skin has an almost glow to it.

Finally, he turns around, his blue eyes narrow. "How long have you been standing there?"

"Long enough to know you hate your T-shirt?"

"I don't hate anything. Hate means weakness." What the heck sort of answer is that? "And you're late."

I look down at my phone. "No, I've been standing here three minutes."

He smirks. "That long then?"

"That was trickery," I point out.

"No, that was manipulation." He reaches for another t-shirt on his desk, this one is black and has the logo on the front of it. Soul.

Yes, he is completely sinful.

Full of sin.

If you put his name next to sin in a dictionary, the world would make sense. The universe would applaud, and people would suddenly realize what it really felt like to fall.

I clear my throat. "I'll just put my things in the locker and meet you back out here?"

"You're bartending tonight," he says. "So make sure you—" He tilts his head. "Your makeup looks good, but—" He walks up to me. "May I?"

I frown. "May you what?"

He licks his thumb and presses it against my cheek. "I'm just going to blend it a bit. Since it's so dark in the club if you look more… wrecked, the customers will stare harder. Think of it like more manipulation and trickery. We want them to want to know your story." He smudges the edges of my eyes and tilts my chin toward him.

I don't know why I'm shaking.

Maybe it's fear.

Or maybe it's just because he's singlehandedly one of the most beautiful people I've seen in my life up close.

He also brought me home last night.

And he stayed.

Nobody ever stays.

I clear my throat. "Better?"

He pats me on the head and pauses when my eyes close. I've always loved being touched on my head, I have no clue why and if I had parents that were still alive, I'd ask them about it, but I'm assuming it's a familiar thing that makes me feel safe and loved.

He runs his large hand up and down.

"Not to disturb whatever this is." Tarek's voice interrupts. "But we have some thirsty customers."

Horus jerks his hand to his side and clears his throat twice. "On my way."

"Yeah, I just have to…" I do a small circle in an attempt to find the employee restroom. "Go."

Tarek points. "Right there, yup, there you go, three steps to your right. What the hell kind of spell did Horus put on you?"

He pets me.

I mean… touched me. He— I shake my head. "Give me one minute."

I don't wait to see what they talk about. I make a beeline toward the employee room, where I shove everything in the first empty locker and close it.

A flash of movement captures my attention.

"What was that?" I ask myself. "Ugh, I'm going crazy."

I look to the right and spot a mirror reflecting my image. I check my face. The smudges near my eyes… I hate that he's right. It looks more mysterious, more high fashion—my makeup.

Who is this guy anyway?

The thought haunts me the entire night, and I swear I can feel his hands still on my head.

For the first time in years—I'm not tired.

I'm alive.

FIVE

自業自得

jigoujitoku

"Self-work, self-profit."

~Japanese proverb

Horus

"**W**hat's a good-looking god of a man like you doing at a place like this, sweetheart?" A woman who, honest to, well um, God, looks like she wants to eat me for breakfast, leans over the bar top, her breasts nearly kissing the small toothpicks by the olives while her hair dangles dangerously close to the beer tap.

A commotion sounds, and then she's getting tapped on the shoulder by Satan, not really but a close second. "Bitch, he's mine. Back off."

It's Alex.

Pretty sure the last thing she's interested in is a washed-up god when a siren related to Ra is standing in front of her. His white and red hair is pulled back into a short ponytail, and strands of that same hair kiss his high cheekbones.

The man could seduce air.

"Oh, um…" She adjusts her tight red dress and self-consciously fluffs up her breasts, then leans against the counter again, almost drunkenly missing it three times before laughing like the inability to stand is hilarious. "You're beautiful too."

"I know." Alex smiles. "But I'm taken by that big chunk of man over there you've been hitting on."

"Alex…" I grind out his name as my teeth clench.

Alex winks at me. "Baby, it's fine! We live in modern times, just embrace the fact that you like it when I—"

"Why are you here?" I interrupt.

The drunken lady starts swaying to the music. Alex sighs and points her toward the dance floor. "Go, go, go, go."

She stumbles off and grabs onto a demon.

"That won't end well." I cringe as the soulless demon—one of the few beings without souls in the club—clutches onto her and starts whispering in her ear, his eyes burning red.

"Meh, he'll just get drunk really fast, she'll sober up, and we'll make sure he doesn't completely wreck her life."

"We?" I repeat.

"Surprise!" Stephanie pops out of nowhere, dragging poor Cassius through the crowd. His jet-black hair hangs past his shoulders, and his blue eyes scan the room like he's already planning on having to work tonight. The guy has no clue how to blend in. Then again, I'm not much better. He's wearing a black T-shirt that says "bite me" with full vampire fangs on it, ripped jeans, and he looks seconds away from tearing a demon's head from his body.

"Ethan got him that shirt for his birthday," Alex says proudly. "I got him the really cool mermaid cuff on his right hand."

"It's pink."

"Bastard pulled off the feather I glued to it." Alex pouts.

I tilt my head toward him. "Why would you glue a feather to his bracelet?"

Alex smirks at me. "Because it tickles, and when something brings pleasure and mirth to one area, it makes you more susceptible to pleasure in other areas. Really, it was a birthday present for him and a present for Stephanie, if you get my meaning."

"No," I deadpanned, "I don't."

"Sex." He throws up his hands. "The act of sex and sexual desire. If you've never used a feather, you're missing out. Just the lightest of teasing touches and *bam*!"

I jump as he claps his hands aggressively in front of me. "How unfortunate for him that he removed it."

"Between you and me, I think he removed it to use it on her—"

"What can I get you to drink?" I say quickly.

Frowning thoughtfully, Alex gives me a side-eyed stare. "You're a god. You should be completely comfortable with the act of lovemaking."

I sigh and look away. "Yeah, well, if you haven't noticed, it's been a while. Kind of stuck in a weird future time loop, so really, when you do the math…"

Alex's eyes widen. "How are you alive? Are you okay? Because if you need something to take the edge off, I can seduce whoever you want to come over here and be of service to you."

I shake my head slowly. "I'm good, but thanks for the offer."

He spreads his arms wide. "The menu's nice tonight."

I think he means the women, but the last people I want to have, er, relations with are humans at this point.

Mainly because they seem too dumb and every time I get hit on, they think showing me tight clothes and skin means intelligence.

Nothing challenges me in this world.

Nothing.

How depressing.

"Drink?" I repeat.

"Peppermint schnapps." Alex winks.

I make a face. "Gross."

"Hope likes it," he says before turning and facing his wife, who just walked in the bar. She takes one look at him and sprints into his arms, tackling him against the counter, her mouth fused with his.

They're like that on a daily basis. I've never been so thankful to live outside of the immortal compound. Ethan's mansion is huge, and typically if you're on the Immortal Council, you stay there in case of emergencies or a lockdown, but the minute I noticed all the happy couples, I realized I would rather face my dad Osiris again than spend one more night hearing everyone having sex.

"Hope?" I hand Alex his drink. "The usual?"

She shakes her head. "Water's good."

I pause.

Her brown eyes crinkle at the sides.

I slide my hand across the bar top and grab her by the wrist, my thumb brushing against her pulse. Tiny little flutters make themselves known against my skin.

There's a cadence of two.

I can't hold my smile back. "Congratulations."

Alex turns back to us. "It's not her birthday."

I snort out a laugh. "He doesn't know?"

Hope lifts her water glass to me and winks. "Cheers, I guess?"

"Know what?" Alex looks dumbly between us. "Hey, why aren't you drinking white wine? It's her favorite, worst bartender ever."

"She's pregnant, dumbass." Cassius jerks out a barstool and plops down onto it. I'm surprised it doesn't break under his weight. "Any idiot could tell. Are you sure you have Ra's blood in you?"

"Smelled her from the door." Timber appears suddenly behind Cassius. "Looks like the siren's having a panic attack." He kicks a barstool over. Alex collapses onto it, his face pale. "This might be the best day of my life."

I laugh when Alex shakily reaches for his peppermint schnapps and starts chugging while the girls fall into easy conversation.

Tarek pops up next to me and slides a beer toward Timber. "Who's pregnant?"

Hope raises her hand.

He sniffs the air. "Wow, good luck, Alex."

Alex simply holds out his hand to me while the rest of the group laughs. "Where's Ethan and Genesis?"

"Vacation." Cassius shrugs. "And Mason went back to Scotland for a bit, so basically, I'm stuck in hell at the mansion with…" He makes a face at Alex. "That one."

"He's not that bad." Stephanie nudges him in the ribs. "Plus, he got you that friendship bracelet."

"It won't come off." His jaw clenches. "And it's a mermaid."

"I may have um… helped charm it," Timber says guiltily. "But since it was a mermaid, I thought it was for Hope, so I wasn't really—"

Cassius jumps to his feet, looking seconds away from obliterating Timber.

"Actually, I think my brother needs me. Behind the bar, far, far away from the angry archangel. Hey, how old are you anyway? Ten thousand? Twenty?" Timber laughs uncomfortably.

"Not helping." Stephanie shoves Timber away.

"Once a demon, always a demon." He salutes Cassius with his middle finger and nearly runs into Kit.

"You're a demon?" she asks.

"One hundred percent accurate," Alex speaks for Timber. "And I'm a male siren. I've been known to—"

Hope elbows him.

"What?" He blinks.

"It's a family joke," Tarek pipes up. "Right, Horus?"

"It's a hilarious one too," I deadpan. "One where this guy crossed an entire desert in nothing but a diaper and his will to live. Woke up with sand in every crevice, lost his memory, probably shit his pants, sound accurate Timber?"

I can feel his irritation.

He wants to punch me.

Hey, it's been over a thousand years since I could tease the god of the underworld, and it's deserved when it comes to this guy. Plus, he did abandon me for true love, as if that's something special.

Maybe I've lived too long.

Timber holds up a finger. "First, I wasn't in a diaper—"

Cassius leans forward. "Actually, ancient Egyptians used

to wear a clothlike…" He reads the room and clears his throat. "It's my birthday."

Timber glares. "Forgiven."

"Are these your friends?" Kit laughs.

"Family." Timber eyes me up and down. "Can't you see the resemblance in the good looks, the bright blond hair, and those eyes?"

She shrugs. "Sure?" She ignores the pull of all the immortals as if they have zero effect on her and turns to me. "Some guy puked in the men's restroom then actually did shit his pants since he clearly didn't have an Egyptian diaper on him. Can you send someone to clean it up?"

"Not it," Tarek says quickly.

Timber's stare is wicked. "I'm the owner of the club, so…"

"We have other waiters," I point out.

Timber grabs me by the shoulders and points me toward the bathroom, whispering in my ear. "Yes, but Ted has trouble tying his shoes and would probably make the situation worse. You, however, have special abilities, so just pop right in there, do a little flick, and come back."

"Why does it feel like Satan's sitting on my shoulder?" I whisper so only he can hear. "And you know we aren't supposed to use our powers flippantly."

Timber slaps me on the ass. "Go, I believe in you."

I roll my eyes and walk by Cassius. "He's your problem now."

Cassius keeps sipping his drink like he's well aware that Timber's his problem.

"But happy birthday," I feel the need to add.

He grumbles something about being too old to be in a club while Timber joins Tarek behind the bar.

Kit's nowhere to be seen when I gain enough courage to go to the men's restroom. I've fought wars. I've faced gods. I've seen kingdoms rise and fall. And I still don't feel prepared for what's behind that metal door.

I take a deep breath and cautiously venture into the bathroom. The stench is so horrible that I almost gag. I can see puke and all the rest of the darkness near the third toilet.

There's a guy lying on the tile floor groaning.

Yeah, well, it's not a fun moment for me either. For being a club, the bathrooms are really nice, with black and white checkered floors, black walls, and mirrors that, if you look at them long enough, hold you captive until a demon can come in and feed on you.

That was Timber's special touch before he actually gained his soul back, though he still keeps them in place so he can control and separate the bad demons from the good.

They think they're about to have a snack all before he judges them and sends them into the underworld.

"Get up," I bark. The guy has puke crusted on his green band T-shirt and can barely keep his eyes open. At least he has pants on.

He ignores me and groans into his hands. "It wasn't supposed to be like this."

"Yeah." I look around the bathroom. "Clearly, your intention was to make it into the toilet, not beside it."

"Not that," he yells, his eyes flashing red. "She doesn't remember me! He promised! Damn it!" He starts banging his head back. "He said all I had to do was give it to her, but she still doesn't remember me!"

Bartender, and now therapist. Have I mentioned I'm stuck in this timeline? Should I remind myself how strange humans are? The man is sitting in his own filth, talking about a woman who doesn't remember him.

I tap my fingertips on the sink and then cross my arms. "There are plenty of hum—women." I correct myself. "Around the dimensions—earth—planet—" Shit. "Seattle." There that's better. "Just be patient and sober up."

A laugh bubbles out of him, and he starts to tug at his hair before pounding the back of his head against the black brick wall. "Nobody"—pound, pound, pound—"Will be like Cat."

My eyes narrow. "You're upset about a missing cat?"

"Are you an idiot?" He glares at me. "Her name was Cat."

"*Was* she a cat?" I'm so confused.

"You're dumb for an adult."

"And you're sitting in your own feces. I think I win this one. Now get up so I can clean you up and send you on your way."

He gets to his feet and stumbles toward me. I hold my breath and snap my fingers, cleaning at least his clothes instantly, not that he would even notice that he suddenly doesn't have puke down his shirt.

"Here!" He throws something that looks like a blue glass marble at my face. I wave my hand in between us to slow both time and the hit. I see the sky in that marble, and it feels so familiar, but I have no idea why.

He's frozen in front of me, locked in his own thoughts and misery. I snatch the glass marble from the air and wave my hand again.

He stumbles forward. "What just happened?"

"You passed out again." I shrug. "The hostess will get you a cab home, all right?"

He stares down at his hands. "I feel like I'm missing something."

I say nothing about the strange marble.

"I lost it again, didn't I? It's not like it worked anyway. She didn't even recognize me."

"Yes, yes, your cat, I know." I turn him toward the door. "Be safe, hydrate, go Hawks."

"I hate football."

"Yup, okay." I shove him out the bathroom door and turn around. With a sigh, I wave my hand carelessly in front of me. The floor's instantly clean, along with the toilet. I refill the paper towels the same way, then turn and look in the mirror only to see Kit's face staring right back at me before she starts to faint.

SIX

出る杭は打たれる

derukui wa utareru

"The nail that sticks out is struck."

~Japanese proverb

Horus

"Shit!" I catch her as she falls into my arms.

Her mouth gapes as her eyes blink up at me.

"Are you okay?"

"Was that magic?"

"Yes." I gulp. "Dark magic, bad puke-killing magic." I try to joke, but her eyes are still unfocused when Cassius walks in, takes one look at me holding Kit, and tilts his head. "Don't ask."

He suddenly sneezes, causing a razor-sharp feather to nearly impale me in the throat before I stop it with my hand.

"Sorry." He winces. "It only happens when I catch a cold."

He is still one percent human, not that I say it out loud.

"Let's get her some air." I pick her up and carry her out of

43

the bathroom, Cassius follows. Timber takes one look at us, his eyes widen like he can sense something went down, and Alex is doing the same thing.

I catch Tarek's gaze. "Take care of the bar; I'll be right back."

"The puke was that bad, huh?" he says with a snicker.

I just nod my head and take the stairs two at a time toward the penthouse apartment over the club.

We always leave the door unlocked because who would dare break in when a god and a werewolf reside here? Demons are dumb, but not that dumb.

That would be death, destruction, and you will never be born again dumb.

Hope and Stephanie follow us into the large living room and start closing the blinds.

Hope's blue eyes flicker with worry from me to the human woman in my arms. I gently lay Kit down on the white leather couch and start to pace. "She saw."

"The poop?" Timber

"Puke?" Cassius offers up.

I'll strangle them both. "No, idiots, she saw me cleaning."

Alex raises his hand. "I have questions."

"Not now!" I yell. "She saw me do this." I slow time, naturally they're fully aware of it, and every single one of them winces.

Cassius sighs. "Easy, we'll just wipe her memory. Won't be the first time, but can I ask why you were using your power to do something a mop could do?"

"So lazy." Timber shakes his head like he's disappointed.

"You!" I jab a finger in his direction.

If he smirks at me one more time, he's dead.

Cassius stands between us. "No fighting. You'll scare her. She's only a human." He taps a finger on his shoulder and winces, pulling a razor-sharp purple and white feather from his skin like he has feathers as scales. He only lets people see them when he wants to, but they're always there, like angelic armor that could kill anyone and anything whenever it wants.

Timber makes a noise in the back of his throat. "That's a big one."

Alex laughs. "That's what she—"

Hope smacks him on the back of the head.

"Sorry," comes his mumble as he rubs the spot she hit.

Cassius hushes everyone. "Quiet." He tosses the feather into the air. It spins around and then blasts across the room, going through all of us before descending onto Kit's forehead.

"What you see isn't true," Cassius says, "but a dream, and when you wake up, you'll remember nothing but fainting."

The purple part of the feather fades into her skin and disappears, leaving nothing but a normal-looking white feather on her face.

Her eyes jolt open.

She covers her mouth with her hand and sits up so fast I'm afraid she's going to pass out again. The normal-looking feather floats on the air down into her lap.

Anyone would think it was from a pillow now, but she picks it up, examines it, and tilts her head up to Cassius. "Is this a magical feather?"

"Nope!" Alex yells, putting his hands in front of him and answering for Cassius. "Magic is a figment of the imagination. A duck wore that feather, a very dumb, ugly, cross-eyed… duck."

"We're…" Cassius glares. "Ghosts."

Alex bursts out laughing, then. "I think I had too much of Cassius's birthday beer, but yeah, sure ghosts with feathers, we'll go with that."

Timber rolls his eyes and walks up to her. "May as well." He points his finger at her chest and tethers her soul, frowning when it's not blue like every other human's.

It's orange.

"Ummmm. Problem."

Alex raises his hand. "Ummm… questions?"

Cassius shakes his head. "Is that orange?"

"Are you blind?" Timber yells. "Hurry and wipe her memory again!"

"You're the idiot who checked her soul!" Cassius shoves him out of the way and plucks another feather, trying to do the same thing.

Kit's visibly shaking when he puts the feather against her head again. "What makes you think it's going to work now when it didn't work before?" she asks.

The room goes silent.

Cassius drops his hand.

Timber takes a step back in front of the girls while Alex's eyes blaze gold. He holds out his hands like a shield. "What are you?"

Kit's teeth start to chatter as she pushes to her feet. "Wh-what do you mean what am I? What are *you?*"

"Ghosts probably isn't the answer right now," I mutter under my breath.

A tear slides down her cheek. "Are you going to kill me?"

"We don't barbecue human," Alex says unhelpfully. "We prefer chicken."

"I do like a good duck every so often," Timber just has to add.

"I don't disagree with that statement," Alex admits.

The door to the apartment opens. Ethan, vampire lord, is standing at the entrance in all his glory, fangs descending past his lower lip, wearing a lumberjack-style red flannel shirt and ripped jeans. "I heard yelling."

"At your house ten miles away?" Timber asks.

"Not you." His gaze lands on Kit. "You."

"Me?" She starts crying in earnest. "What is this? What are you?"

"You guys haven't even told her? What the hell is going on?" Ethan charges in and shakes his head at all of us, his expression one of pure disbelief. "You can't just—" He sniffs the air. "Why are you holding a human hostage?"

"Why do you call me human?" she asks, voice weak.

"This isn't going well," I say, more to myself than anything. "Cassius, you should be able to wipe her memory."

Kit retreats a step, covering her mouth in horror and speaking through her fingers. "Can't I keep my memories?"

Timber waves a hand across her face and stumbles backward. "She's empty."

"That's rude," Hope says under her breath.

"No, I mean..." He waves his hand again, probably freaking Kit out even more. "She's empty. There aren't any conscious memories."

I quickly shove him out of the way and snap my fingers in front of her face. "SLEEP!"

She collapses in my arms, and the room around us goes eerily silent.

Cassius presses a hand to her forehead. "I haven't seen an orange soul in centuries."

I swallow the lump in my throat. "The ancient Chinese and Japanese had orange souls when they worshipped the creatures of the forest for protection, and some were turned immortal as a gift for living a good life, but it still doesn't explain why a plain human would have one."

"I got nothing." Timber shakes his head. "Is she here on purpose? I sense nothing wrong with her soul. She just has the strange mark of color."

"There's nothing to fix. It's just an odd color."

"She's not human," Cassius finally says.

"Maybe not her soul, but her body is," Timber clarifies.

I lay her gently back on the couch. "Let her rest before we start asking questions."

"Or we start now." Ethan takes a step forward, fangs descending again. "Blood never lies."

"Ethan." Cassius moves in front of him.

Ethan shoves him out of the way. "We're the Immortal Council. Our job is to protect humanity and keep the balance with immortals. I'll have a small taste and see if I can find anything of her past."

"Just don't get stuck there," Timber mutters under his breath. "Am I right, Horus?"

I flip him off.

"Ah, too soon, too soon." Alex slaps Timber on the shoulder. "I hope you know what you're doing, Ethan. The last thing you need is to be sucked into whatever has her soul captive right now because it sure as hell is powerful and ancient."

"He's ancient," Alex murmurs.

"Yeah, okay, demi-god." Ethan drops to his knees. His fangs descend and bite right into her neck as a nightmarish scream from the pit of hell escapes from between her lips.

And I swear for a second.

I see orange fur on her hands.

SEVEN

見ぬが花

minu ga hana

"Not seeing is a flower," "Reality is never as good as your imagination"

~Japanese proverb

Horus

Her eyes roll into the back of her head as red blood runs down Ethan's mouth, dripping onto the white couch. She starts yelling in Japanese, and even though I'm a god, my territory was always Egypt. I know English, I know Farci, Hebrew, Greek, and Armenian. I can read Hieroglyphics. But I never left the ancient world; doing so was never my purpose or calling.

Ethan stumbles back, his eyes glowing green. "Past lives."

I almost roll my eyes. "Everyone has past lives, vampire."

"Not like this." He shakes his head. "Not even close. She's been thrust into eternal purgatory, a loop of loneliness."

Timber grunts. "I think I know what that used to be like."

"And you call us your friends," Alex grumbles. "So, where's her origin? Egypt? Greece? Seems to be the theme here, some great powerful, wonderful immortal made a really poor life choice or mistake, lost their power, had them shielded…" The guy actually yawns. "Is she a lesser god trapped in a human body?" He mimics playing a tiny violin. "Figure it out so we can fix it, so it doesn't cause damage to her human body or soul or—" He checks his watch. "Be right back. I need a sandwich."

Ethan lunges toward him, but Cassius stops him in his tracks and shakes his head. "Sometimes it's easier when he's not present for group projects."

Ethan wipes his face and spits blood onto the floor.

I sigh and look down. "That's a new area rug."

Timber nudges me. "How do you even know what that is?"

"Do not follow his TikTok," Cassius warns.

I roll my eyes. "Can we talk about the problem at hand? We've hired some sort of"—I point at her—"something, but she needs our help."

Cassius crosses his arms. "Heaven wouldn't tell me even if I begged. Our job is to fix, and their job is to watch."

Have I mentioned how much I hate the no-intervening rule?

I guess now that my powers are limited, it's not like I could truly do a ton other than make her levitate, see visions, or help restore her soul and memories, but I have no way of doing that if I don't know what she is.

"She's of Japanese descent," I muse aloud, but mostly to myself. "When The Watchers fell, the twelve brothers were sent to the twelve corners of the earth in order to earn forgiveness for the rest of the fallen while they suffer in the Abyss."

I swear I can hear Alex roll his eyes as he yells from the kitchen, "Trust me, we know, we're kind of on the same team now, got one of them on the council, the other knits sweaters for the homeless—we're covered in that arena."

"Except one," Cassius whispers.

I frown. "There's one missing?"

"Oh no, Alex knows exactly where he is," Timber says. "It's more or less getting there, and getting him to talk, which I highly doubt he'd actually do since he tried to destroy the world and, oh yeah, kill all of us, mainly Alex. But can you really blame him?"

"Bannik," Cassius whispers his name like a curse.

Meanwhile, Kit lies there, nearly motionless, her hands draped at her sides, her skin pale, tiny specks of blood drying to her lifeless neck.

I don't know her, but in the last few hours, I feel like we've traumatized her for life, she's going to wake up and scream monsters, and she'll be right because this won't make sense without her memories.

Bannik's name is familiar; he was the angel who condemned Archangel and Watcher Sariel for sleeping with a human, for forgetting his place and his purpose in life. That caused a great hatred between Bannik and the woman whose son is currently standing in front of me.

Cassius. A Dark One. Half human, half angel, until his father sacrificed his power to Cassius and ascended back from where he came.

Where I help rule.

The sky.

It shook the immortal realm. What did one actually do with a half-human half-angel who had all of the knowledge of the heavens and all of the failings of an imperfect perfection? Constantly pulled in two directions, constantly wanting to return to their origin but lusting for what human life provides.

No god ever envied Cassius.

And now that I know him personally, I realize that maybe the world would have been a better place had we all had people who followed their hearts despite the ramifications. Otherwise, how else would we have a king of the immortals like Cassius?

I'm sure that one percent part of him that's human still causes the rest of him to struggle, but at least now the Creator smiles down on him and the rest of us—for now.

Unless something happens.

I know that's why he's always so diligent.

"He was the one closest to my father," Cassius whispers. "The one who warned him, who resented him for losing his position of power." He sighs. "Bannik has no traces of good left in him; believe me when I say that."

"None," Alex agrees, as he takes a huge bite of the sandwich. "Last I heard he was in The Abyss yelling at everything that walked by him, and it's not like he's in a dark cave by himself; there's tons of people there."

I take all this in and think for a moment. Then, "And he was in charge of which human plane, exactly?"

The room goes silent.

Timber speaks first, his voice low. "Asia."

"So basically, the only one who would have any semblance of information is currently rotting in the Abyss and hates everyone in this room?" I ask.

"Yup." Ethan seems calmer; he shoves his hands in his pockets. "So until then, we'll just guard her, make sure she's safe. Obviously, she's not in any external danger. She's in more danger from us than she is from anything else that could threaten her."

"So we just live with this mystery and her suffering?" I ask.

Cassius frowns at me. "What else do you want us to do? Our hands are tied. Besides, you're working with her; you can keep an eye on her and report back. Think of it as your second job."

"I never wanted a first," I growl low in my throat.

Timber slaps me on the shoulder. "But the uniform looks really nice on you."

"If you weren't the god of the underworld, I'd kill you," I hiss over at him.

He smirks and holds up his hands. "Sorry, I know this is a hard adjustment for you not to be able to just snap your fingers, but try to behave and make sure that nothing strange happens to her. Oh, and don't let any demons near her soul. If they find out how ancient it is, they'll kill each other to grab it." He looks around the room. "I'd let her stay here tonight since she'll be out a while. Then you can be the one to explain to her what happened." He slaps me on the shoulder. "Good luck."

Timber starts walking off with Stephanie and Hope, who both give me odd little smiles. Cassius follows with Ethan, but Alex hangs back.

"What?" I ask.

He finishes off his sandwich and then shrugs. "I kind of want to stay to watch the shit show of you attempting to explain all of this before she runs away screaming."

"Out." I point at the door.

He shoves his empty plate into my hands. "Yup."

What? As if I can't talk to a human?

Laughable.

I put the plate in the strange thing that washes the dishes, then I settle in on one of the large chairs and wait for her to wake up.

EIGHT

七転び八起き

Nanakorobi yaoki

"Stumbling seven times but standing up eight"

However many setbacks you face, never give up and always keep trying.

-Japanese proverb

Kit

I dream of the forest and the moonlight, of cuddling with someone who has warm hands and deep laughter, but my dream quickly disappears into a nightmare. I remember going to sleep so content and happy one minute, then screaming through the forest, running, and falling as something wrapped around my ankle, dragging my body across the hard soil. I hit the bumps over and over again, digging my nails into the cold hard dirt before I'm pulled into a dark cave.

"What will you trade?"

I look up at the darkness and hear the sound of hissing, but I don't live near a place native to large snakes.

At least, I don't think so.

"I have nothing of value," I finally admit, knowing death is coming. The stench of rotting corpses is so strong, surely my time to join them is next.

She laughs. "I don't need money."

I stare out of the mouth of the cave at the moonlight trickling in. "I don't even have someone to give you."

My family is gone.

The warmth was stolen from me, or maybe I just got lost? I cannot remember anything but the warmth and then the stark reality of cold.

"I value… treasure," she finally says. "What are you willing to exchange with me for your life?"

"You'll spare me if I exchange?" I whimpered, already bleeding all over the place, and not sure how I even got the bruises already.

More dark laughter. "Of course. Shall I take your pretty hair? Maybe a tail?"

Tail? What tail?

I say nothing.

She snaps her fingers. "I've got it! If you truly want to trade what's most precious, then if you survive—which I hope you do—the three tests and manage to make it through until the end, I'll give what's most precious to you back.

I still have no clue what that is. I stay silent.

"Now," the mesmerizing female voice whispers, "open your pretty little mouth."

I hesitate.

A low hum builds up in my throat, making it impossible to keep my mouth closed. My lips part and something is pulled from my body, something necessary. It is everything important to me. I know this the minute it starts leaving me.

It is memories.

It is my life.

It is everything that makes me, me.

And it is gone in a flash of light, leaving me alone, naked in the darkness of that cave, wondering where I am, who I am, and wishing someone would just tell me so I can go to sleep.

Tears stream down my face as my eyes flicker open, and I stare up at Horus. He doesn't look concerned so much as curious.

I quickly sit up and swipe at my cheeks. "How long was I out?"

"A while." He hands me a mug of hot tea. I take it instantly and drink it, then start to choke, remembering all the weird things I saw before passing out.

Horus stays still and silent. Maybe he's waiting for me to ask or burst into tears, scream, and run away.

I glance at the door. It's partially opened. And then it fully opens when a gorgeous man with jet-black hair and green eyes strolls in. He takes one look at me, cocks his head to the side, and frowns. "Is she broken? She's not even screaming?"

The sound of someone eating chips breaks the silence before another voice speaks. "Maybe she is broken." It's one of the beautiful guys from the bar, and he brings out chips and salsa and sets them on the coffee table. "I'm missing House of the Dragon for this."

"You'll live," the other hot guy says before sitting across from me in a large leather chair. "I'm Ethan."

Horus looks irritated. "Didn't I tell you guys to leave?"

I shakily look from Horus to both guys, then focus on Ethan. Something about his eyes pulls me in.

"H-hi, Ethan, I'm Kit." I don't hold out my hand; something tells me deep in my soul that it would be dangerous to do so.

The corners of his mouth lift into a seductive smile. "Interesting, she's not afraid, but her mind tells her she needs to be." He flashes seriously long fangs and then leans forward. "What do you remember?"

My throat is dry, so I drink more tea before I answer. "Magic. Horus doing magic, and then you guys trying to erase memories or something, and then a lot of pain. I had a weird dream about a cave and woke up on the couch."

"Good." He nods. "I'm just here to grab this one." He pulls the other guy up from the chair and shoves him toward the door. "He's like a disease you can't cure. You'd be stuck with him all night." He looks over his shoulder. "Have fun, Horus. Try not to scare her too much."

"I'm not scary," Horus grumbles.

He's huge.

Beautiful.

And currently sitting close to me.

Scary? Yes.

Tempting. Even more so.

He clears his throat and motions for me to drink more tea, which I do, then the awkward silence fills with this weird buzz as we stare at each other.

He clears his throat twice and looks away. "I'm not normal."

"Is anyone?"

He smiles down at his massive hands. "Yeah well, I'm a bit more different."

"Werewolf?" I guess trying to amuse myself and keep

myself from freaking out because how was any of this real? My dreams? The reality I just witnessed?

I touch my neck. Nothing's there, but I could have sworn something bit me.

Was it Horus?

Someone else?

The door shuts with a weird finality as I'm stuck with this man sitting in front of me, looking bigger than life.

He gets up. "Not a werewolf."

"Bummer."

His eyes burn freaky bright, I should be scared, but I figure running means he might chase, so I go very still and just wait. "Sorry."

"A mere werewolf?" He laughs. "No, I'm not a werewolf."

"I'm not so sure how that's supposed to make me feel better," I mutter.

He puts his hands on his hips and starts pacing. "Why aren't you running?"

I gulp. "Mainly because I'm hoping it's a bad dream and also because predators chase."

"I haven't chased in centuries." He says it so seriously I'm not sure if he's crazy or if I am.

"Okay." I stand on wobbly legs. "So, what are you?"

He's silent, his eyes narrow. "I don't think you want to know."

"Try me."

"You should eat."

"I have zero appetite after my nightmare and whatever the hell you did in the bathroom and then here in the living room. Plus, I'm exhausted and need to go home."

"No!" he blurts, holding out his hands, then dropping

them. "I mean, you can't go home, you could get hurt."

Fear trickles down my spine. "From whom?"

"It doesn't matter." He shakes his head. "I can protect you here."

"I don't know you!" I clench my fists. "All I know is you did some weird voodoo, and you have weird voodoo friends!"

He smirks. "It's not voodoo, human."

"Stop calling me human!"

"It's what you are!"

"So are you!" I yell.

"NO!" His voice seems to reverberate inside me on a visceral level. He takes a stride toward me and grabs my arm; his eyes burn bright yellow, then gleam sapphire blue. "I'm a god!"

I stumble back and fall onto the couch again. "Your eyes!"

The air around me smells like fresh grass and flowers, and his eyes become blue like the sky. His hands are clenched into fists, and pieces of dirt fall from them onto the floor like he's crushing the earth. The minute the dirt lands, it explodes into a blue star, only to disappear. I wonder if he even realizes he's freaking me the hell out and also doing that.

"Oh, shit!" someone says from the door.

I turn, petrified out of my mind, and see Tarek sipping on a cocktail and shaking his head like he's disappointed. "You can't just go full god on someone like that, Horus. Swear it's like you're the worst managed immortal I've ever seen, and I've seen things, bro, so many things." He sips the rest of his drink and waves with his other hand. "Hey, there."

"Hi." The word squeezes out in a terrified rasp. I don't even lift my hand.

He waves me off. "I got this." He walks over to Horus and snaps his fingers in front of his face, then slaps him. "Wake up, big guy."

Horus shakes his head. His eyes go back to normal, and he stares down at his hands. "Impossible. I'm limited in this timeline."

I raise my hand. "Did someone slip mushrooms into something I ate or drank today?"

"'Shrooms." Tarek laughs. "Classic."

"No, not classic, scared." I point at myself. "Can I go home now and pretend none of this ever happened?"

Horus waves his hand at the door; it shuts and locks.

Tarek grins. "I think that was a no. Not sure, but based on the all-around feel of the room, the look on his face, and the fact that he just slammed the door, you're stuck with an angry god. Good luck, cheers." He freaking starts whistling as he walks off, then enters what must be a bedroom and shuts that door.

"Seriously?" I'm more pissed than scared now.

"That," Horus says, pointing behind him, "was a werewolf." He shakes his head. "Amateur."

"Like I would know!" I yell.

"They are inferior!" He yells right back.

Tarek pokes his head out of the door. "Actually, we're literally the gods of the earth, and I'm a prince. You're the inferior dude who is stuck out of his timeline. Okay, byeeeee."

He closes the door again.

I glance from the door to Horus, then back to the door, then to Horus. "Out of your timeline?"

He runs his hands through his gorgeous blond locks. "It's a long story about saving the world. Care to hear it?"

"You?" I point at him.

He glares. "What do you mean me? Yes, me!"

"You yell a lot."

"You're disrespectful! People used to worship me!"

I snort out a laugh. "Oh, I'm sorry, you were serious."

His skin turns a funny shade of pink. "On your knees."

I laugh. "Oh no, I'm not doing that, even if you are a god."

"I meant in worship, but the alternative doesn't sound so bad either."

I slap him across the face so hard my hand stings, then immediately use the same hands to cover my face, so he doesn't reciprocate.

When nothing happens, I peek through my fingers. He's staring at me, jaw hanging open, eyes wide. "You slapped me."

"You were being rude," I whisper.

He hangs his head, then turns around and mutters, "I need a drink."

I follow him into the modern kitchen. Ignoring me, he grabs a bottle of whiskey, starts chugging it directly, and then puts it down like he's disappointed. "Can't even get drunk here; the best is a light buzz that fades after ten minutes."

"Sorry?"

He looks over his shoulder. "What are you?"

"Human, apparently." I cross my arms.

"You're staying here. You can have my bed, I'll take the couch. But first things first, you get a little history lesson since we can't erase your memories."

"Something tells me this won't be a fun lesson."

"You get spanked if you get answers wrong." He winks.

My entire body buzzes. "Wh-what?"

He breezes by me with his bottle. "You're blushing."

"No! I mean, I was just taken back."

I follow him back into the living room, confused like crazy but unable to leave, afraid to say something wrong, and still under the impression something weird is going on. I mean, obviously, or maybe I've completely lost it.

Wouldn't that be just great?

Horus sits down on the couch. I sit down far away from him on the same couch, he stares down into the whiskey bottle, and his next words might stay with me for the rest of my life. "I'm Horus, the Egyptian god of the sky."

NINE

異体同心
itai doushin
"Two bodies, same heart."
–Japanese proverb

Horus

She looks at me like I'm an idiot.

I don't really know how to respond to that look. Her mouth is slightly parted, her full lips pink and tempting. I just told her I was the god of the sky, and she's staring at me like I'm an idiot.

Her head tilts to the side. "You don't look like a god."

I've never been more offended in my entire existence. "What are gods supposed to look like, I wonder?"

"Bigger." She nods her head. "And don't they glow? Why don't you glow?"

"Why don't *you* glow?" Where has my intelligence escaped to?

"I'm human," she says in a *duh* voice. "And if you're a god, why are you here? What's your purpose?"

I've never had to actually explain myself to someone in all my years of existence, and this measly human needs proof? No, she is *demanding* proof.

I snap my fingers and twist my wrist to the right. The blinds instantly open, and the coffee maker turns on.

She bursts out laughing. "Wow, cool parlor trick."

"What's that? What's a parlor trick? Tarek never showed me those!" Do I need to know them to be relevant? So many questions, and she's still laughing.

She leans forward. "That's easily manipulated. I want to see something unique, O' God of the Sky. Wow, I can't believe I'm having this conversation. Oh damn, maybe I died in the poop bathroom!"

"You're alive, trust me. The poop bathroom was saved by my powers, and I have limited power now that I'm in this timeline, so I can't suddenly do what I've always done, but I can do this," I tether myself to her and jerk her forward. She slams against my chest, her hands spread against my T-shirt. "How's that?"

"Your heartbeat," she whispers, her fingers drumming against my chest in a perfect cadence. "It's so fast."

"All gods have faster heartbeats, we live longer, we're faster, we're created differently than humans."

"Are you calling me lazy?"

"I'm calling you weak, but lazy works too."

She shoves my chest.

I don't even move.

"Let me guess, you're really strong too?"

I nod. "I thought it was obvious."

"And arrogant, lucky me."

"Stay here tonight," I say again. "And I'll make you breakfast in the morning."

She huffs out a breath. "So what? You're a god, he's a werewolf, and I'm guessing the other dude was like a vampire or something?"

"Male siren, vampire, archangel, goddess, fairy…" I shrug. "Take your pick, we're all from different races, but we work together to make sure humanity survives."

This time her mouth really does stay open in shock. I almost close it when she lets out a shriek. "This can't be real! I just haven't slept in days! You know that's how it works, right? This stupid insomnia paired with nightmares. I'm off my sleep meds; yup, that's what this is. I just can't seem to snap out of it. Hurry up, pinch me, or hit me."

"I don't hit women, I don't pinch them unless it's their nipples or ass, and I highly doubt you're in the mood for that. Why don't you go take a shower, and I'll grab you some fresh clothes?"

"Are you cleaning me to eat me?"

I grin and lean down. "Do you want me to eat you?"

Her eyes flash.

Interesting.

A rush of lust punches me in the chest and travels south. "No. Never."

"Liar." I tug her earlobe. "But you're cute when you lie, so I'll let it slide."

"Ughhhh!' She starts off in the wrong direction to the bathroom, then turns around and walks back.

"I knew where I was going."

I nod. "I believe you."

The bathroom door slams.

And I'm left smiling and thanking Timber for forcing my hand.

TEN

人を信じよ、しかし、その百倍も自らを信じよ

Hito o shinjiyo, shikashi, sono hyaku-bai mo mizukara o shinjiyo

Believe in people, but believe in yourself a hundred times more.

~Osamu Tezuka, Japanese manga artist and animator

Kit

Weirdest night of my life.

With the most beautiful man I've ever seen in the absolute strangest circumstances I've ever been in.

I pinch the skin on my arm again. Nope, still awake, still here. Spending the night with a god. I tried to play it cool, but internally I was dying with curiosity and wonder.

People worshipped him for good reason, didn't they?

And more importantly, why did they stop?

I splash water onto my face, try to get myself under control, then grab my hair tie and pull my hair back. When

I stare at myself in the mirror, I feel lost, like I should know who I am but have no clue where I started or where I will eventually end. I'm like this empty thing. My brown eyes stare back at me, clueless, and my brown hair, with its shots of red on the bottom, lay there against my chest. I wonder what would happen if I had powers… powers I could make come alive and help me. I want power. Why am I hungry for it? Why does it seem like the next best thing other than just acceptance but pulling in every source of energy I have?

I open my hands, my palms sting. Yes. This feels right. But also so wrong. I feel like I'm going to puke. My hands grip the porcelain countertop. What just happened?

A sudden pang hits my chest. I touch it with my fingertips. What am I missing? Why do I feel like something is so lost?

So lost.

Lost.

Lost.

I can't find it.

I gave it away.

But what did I give?

I crumple to my knees; they hit the hard tile, making a crunching noise I know will haunt me later. One that will tell me that my knees are strained again, that my health is bad, all because of things I don't understand and things I've lost but can't find.

I quickly jump to my feet and grab a towel, washing the wetness from my face, and stare at myself one more time in the mirror. Is it normal, I wonder, to look at yourself and not see yourself? But a stranger? It's why I've always avoided mirrors because it feels wrong, it feels *other*.

My eyes feel right, but my face feels wrong.

I'm crazy.

It's the only reason I can't sleep, the only reason I don't recognize myself, and why nobody really sees me.

I hold onto the counter to keep myself from a repeat fall to the floor. My brain is dizzy again; it always gets this way when I feel sorry for myself, when I just... *want.*

I want love.

I want someone to hold me, but more than that, I want them to tell me to fight, but for what? What do I have to fight for?

Nobody thinks of me. Nobody cares.

I smile to myself. It's a sad smile.

I tell myself it's okay.

And then I walk out of the bathroom in a trance and head toward Horus, this god who doesn't care if I live or die, this god who claims to be all of these things.

Funny how you wake up in a world that isn't your own, only to realize that nobody is here to save you. They're here to condemn you.

I take a deep breath and step into the living room. He's sitting there, looking gorgeous, holding his hands together, gripping them like he's nervous.

That makes two of us.

"I'm going to try to sleep," I say.

He doesn't even look over his shoulder. "Good idea."

"Perfect," I add. "I'm going to just take the couch."

"No!" he barks and jumps to his feet. "You'll take the bed; I already put on fresh sheets, come."

I open my mouth to protest, but the way he's looking at me is more terrifying than anything I've ever seen in my life—at least as far as I'm aware—so I meekly follow him into the bedroom. He has a little salt lamp next to his bed and its pinkish-orange glow beckons. The sheets are pulled back in an invitation to seek rest. Enough pillows are piled on the bed to suffocate me and ten others. And I choked up a little as I notice that he put a bottle of water on the nightstand.

"So, yeah," he says, waving his hand in front of me. "Try to get some rest."

"Yeah." I nod, the tiniest bit shocked at his efforts. "I'll do that."

"Good." He stands there, staring at the bed, then starts to leave, and I have no clue why I do it, but I reach out and grab his wrist.

He stills. "What are you doing?"

"I don't know."

He clenches his hand.

"Please," I whisper. "Stay."

Why do his blue eyes seem sad? He grips my forearm and turns it over as though he's looking for something; his thumb rubs down my skin, and it burns so good I almost sigh. "I like that."

"You shouldn't," he whispers.

"Can you stay?" I ask. "Can I?"

He sighs deeply. "Just don't touch me."

When his hand grips mine, I feel complete. I don't know how to explain it, but it's hard to breathe as he pulls me the rest of the way into his bedroom. His bed is massive. I sit on the edge, and Horus gently pulls back the sheets and then tucks me in.

The bed dips a little as he settles next to me.

I hate that I'm upset because he stopped holding my hand. I feel empty again, sick to my stomach. I curl up on my side.

"If you could have anything," he says quietly, "anything in the world, what would it be?"

Tears burn the backs of my eyes before I answer softly, "A friend."

He seems to startle at that, or maybe it's my imagination. "You don't have friends?"

"I have me." My voice shakes. I can't believe I'm telling him this, but I feel out of control, and right now, I just need someone to tell me it's okay, it's all going to be okay. I can't remember anything, and on top of that, I just had a traumatic experience with gods and immortals, and who the hell knows what else.

Why can't they help me?

Suddenly frustrated, I turn around and glare at him. He's lying next to me, peaceful. Calm. How the HELL dare he?

"Why!" I yell.

Horus jerks back and nearly falls off the bed. "What the hell?"

"Why!" I yell again. "If you're a god and I'm a human, why do I have to suffer? I've done everything right! I've tried so freaking hard, but why? Why am I suffering? Why do *you* get the power? Why do I get to sit here and cry? Why? I want to know why my tears fall. I want to know why I have no memories of love. I want to know why. WHY!"

I don't realize I'm sobbing until I can't see.

He slowly raises his hands and rests them on my shoulders, then pulls me against his chest. I sob until I can't breathe.

"I have no excuses," he whispers. "I have no answers to the Creator's reasons for pain, but I do have this."

"What?" I sob. "A magic pill to make me forget?"

His smile is sad. "Not so much." His head lowers, but he hesitates as if he doesn't understand the words coming out of his mouth but feels compelled to say them. "One thing given to all gods that can't be taken away."

"What's that?" I sniffle.

His smile is full of something I don't think I can even categorize as he lowers his head and brushes his lips against mine. "Love."

"You don't love me. You don't know me."

"But I can show you love; any being can show love if, even for an instant, they can at one moment choose to love someone over themselves, choose to be selfless for a small amount of time. Every single second that passes, we are given a choice, and if you use those seconds for others, knowing that you will never get that time back, is that not love?"

I feel like I've heard these words before.

I open my mouth to protest, yet I know he's right. Sacrifice is love. Even if all you're sacrificing is time.

I nod my head. "Then give me love, just for a few seconds."

"And if I choose to give you a minute?"

"Then you're a very benevolent god, aren't you?"

"I was." He frowns. "I am."

ELEVEN

振り向くな、振り向くな、後ろには夢がない
Furimuku na, furimuku na, ushiro ni wa yume ga nai
Don't look back, don't look back, there is no dream in the back.
~Shuji Terayama, Japanese playwright and poet

Horus

She's staring up at me like I've lost it, and I'm staring down at her like I've finally found something I've been searching for, for a thousand years, maybe more. I've always given of myself; it's part of the job. But for some reason, I don't feel like I'm doing her a favor by touching her; it's like she's doing me a favor by allowing it. Everything inside of me warms. My own soul starts to reach out, tapping pieces of my heart with its tentacles, warming me.

Her hypnotic green eyes lock onto me with anticipation and maybe a bit of fear.

Adrenaline surges through my system, and my brain tells me that if I just touch her, everything in my world and hers will finally make sense.

Is this what love is?

77

Is this just a connection?

I want to protect her and, at the same time, let her protect herself and fight for herself.

I don't know what to do, so I simply just lower my head and wonder what happens next.

Her hands cup the sides of my head. "Love?"

"Love," I whisper back. "I've never experienced it."

"And now?"

"Now I feel something. I feel protective." I frown. "For no reason. I've only ever given myself out of kindness, never out of my own personal need or want." I don't know her. I just want her. I want to protect her. I feel like I've known her for a thousand years.

And I desire her. It must be the timeline, the way I've lost some of my powers that has me wishing to do carnal things, that has my mind tricked that she's the answer to everything.

A kiss doesn't solve problems. Oftentimes it leads to them, so why does it feel like the opposite with this pretty stranger I shouldn't even be touching?

Despite my own warnings, I still want to give her these seconds, maybe minutes, so I press my lips to her mouth and immediately feel a force shove me back against the wall.

I'm held there.

Motionless and nearly unable to breathe as the force holds me still.

She passes out on the bed while my vision blackens.

And I finally see. I finally know.

"Stop!" She laughs and shoves against me. A thousand years ago seems like yesterday. "Remember, we aren't supposed to be together. The heavens would be livid!"

I laugh and splash her with more water from the lake. "What can they do? I'm a god… you're a goddess…"

"Yeah, a lesser goddess to you."

I shrug. "Who cares? Just be with me."

"Be with me."

Thunder strikes overhead. I think nothing of it. I can protect her from anything in our world. But it keeps coming until rain starts pelting from above. We dress and hide under one of the trees.

"Love her and lose yourself, your family, but by all means, bring the start of chaos and ending of worlds to fruition," a female voice says.

I stall. "Who's there?"

"Medusa." She laughs. "Apophis." Another laugh erupts from what feels like the depths of The Abyss itself. "You choose. Either way, I'm chaos, and you're really ruining my plans."

I shove my love behind me. "It doesn't matter."

"Oh, but it does."

She peers around me at Kit. "What would you sacrifice for him?"

I frown, and then I can't breathe. She's gripping my throat so hard that I can't even get the words out to tell her that this demon can't kill me. She can't, I'm too powerful, but Kit doesn't know she's a lesser goddess. I move my hands.

"Awww…" She clenches my throat harder. "How sad, the love of your life… and all I really want is one thing…"

Kit straightens. "Let him go, and we'll talk."

She drops me to the ground. "Easy. Done. One day I will collect; you better hope your god is there when I do."

I wake up in a cold sweat and stumble toward the bathroom.

My shift at the bar starts in an hour. Was I sleeping? Dreaming? Sleepwalking? I glance around the room. Kit's nowhere to be found. The sound of water fills the small apartment, and then she's coming out of the bathroom.

"Oh!" She grins, passing me on the way to the kitchen. "You're finally up! You must have been tired last night because you completely passed out on the couch. Want eggs?"

Eggs? Do I want eggs? And why did I dream what I had?

"Yeah, um, sure." I scratch my head and sit up. Maybe it really was a horrible dream.

"Good, I'm great at eggs, terrible at everything else."

I frown. "Do you remember last night?" I ask.

She pauses, her hand resting on the carton of eggs before she looks over her shoulder. "It was a long night, I mean, yeah I remember, but we were both tired, let's just work and train today, okay? I want to say no. I want to scream it. Instead, I say, "Okay."

I get ready.

I eat her eggs.

And I train her like it's every other day, still wondering what she is, what my part in her life is, and wondering why I had a nightmare as if we were already together.

"Horus," Kit runs up to me. "The guy back there grabbed my ass, and I kicked him. I didn't mean to, but it was like instinct—"

"I'll end him."

"No." She presses her hands against my chest. "Like I said, I already kicked him in the balls, but like, is there protocol for this? Should I call the cops?"

I want to say I am the cops.

Instead, I suck in a deep breath. "I'll take care of it. Just make sure you…" I look her up and down. "Stop looking so attractive."

"It's a T-shirt." She rolls her eyes.

I grab her by the wrist and jerk her close to me. "It. Is. *Tempting.*"

"Even to you?"

I can hardly breathe. "You don't see yourself the way others see you. I would devour you in one second, then come back for more." I huff out an annoyed breath. "Wear a sweater."

Aren't ugly sweaters a thing? A funny little thing with humans these days? I have no clue why.

I release her, feeling kind of guilty yet satisfied as I approach the table of men still laughing. I cross my arms. "Who's first?"

The guys all stare me down like they're about to breathe their last breath. I stand there with my arms crossed, just waiting to see who's going to shit themselves first, when I hear the sound of a siren.

How the hell did any cops get here so fast?

I look over my shoulder at Kit, she gives me a guilty look.

I slam my hands down on the table, causing all of the men to fall out of their chairs. It breaks along with the glass that falls to the floor. I don't kill anyone, but the desire is there. "Don't." I hiss through my teeth. "Touch anyone, man or woman, in this bar without their consent, or I'm going to pull your spleen through your mouth and feed it to the demons in the back while I tether your soul to Hell. Understand?"

An officer walks up to me. "Did they do this?"

"I don't know." I look at the first man. "Did you?"

He nods his head emphatically. "It was a violent rage. Thank God this man was here to calm us down."

I smirk at the water running down his pant leg onto his shoe. Yes, thank me all you want; that stupid human's lucky to still have a working cock.

"All right, we just have a few questions." He turns to me. It's going to be a long day already.

I participated in all the questioning, and by the time I was done, I was exhausted just attempting to act normal and not violent.

She's so pretty.

I tell myself it's because it's been so long and because she's a strong person whose identity I can't figure out.

It's curiosity.

She's not human, and yet she is.

I'm completely clueless as a god, something that's never happened. Maybe, it's going to be fine, maybe I'll just guard her the rest of my life, and she will live long and happy with someone other than me.

Oh hi, hello, nice to see you again, I'm Horus, and that girl's really pretty, and I'll never get to kiss her again.

Fuck.

I toss the rag against the counter and lean against it.

"Humans," Tarek says. "Am I right?"

"Why are you here again?"

He frowns. "I work here?"

"Right, but why don't you go home to Scotland and just… rule or do what werewolves do?"

"Ohhh, that." He laughs. "I have a job outside of that, I'm currently doing it, but damn, my clients be hard to crack."

"Huh?"

"What?"

"Did you say something?"

"I yawned?" He literally fakes a yawn. "Anyway, just keep going with it. Plus, you never know what might happen when you decide to save something other than yourself."

He's looking at Kit.

"She's human," I say. "She'll be fine."

"She's both," he corrects. "And she must be very tired. Exhausted actually. I wonder what you're willing to sacrifice in order to save her."

"What?"

"Figure it out, Horus, god of the sky." He nods toward me.

And I spend the rest of the night wondering what the hell he's talking about. The only person who truly would know what she is, is in the Abyss, and I'm not about to go against everything and travel down there to save some stranger who I don't even know.

I laugh. Right. I would never do that. Ever. I'm a god. She's clearly lesser, no matter what.

I'm not stupid.

I would never.

Ever.

Her laughter echoes around the bar.

Ever.

Ever.

I squeeze my eyes shut.

So why does it feel so familiar? The way her laugh carries around the room? And the way I crave it like my next breath.

TWELVE

酒は本心を表す
sake wa honshin wo arawasu
"Sake shows true feelings."
-Japanese proverb

Kit

I hate taking out the trash. I don't know if it's because it's heavy or if it's just me being grumpy, but I do it anyway. I take the giant black trash bag out back and toss it in the enormous dumpster.

The lid slaps down with a thud. "There."

I turn to go back into the door leading to the club and see someone standing there, smoking a cigarette. He takes another puff, then tosses it to the ground and steps on it. "You want to be free?"

"No," I answer immediately. "I want to go back to my job so I can make rent."

He snickers. He's wearing a green trench coat and black boots, he has no shirt on beneath his coat, and his head is covered in a black beanie; all I see are green eyes and a smirk.

"I think you should come back with me. I mean, if you don't finish this last life, what really was the purpose of jumping?"

"Jumping?" I repeat. "When did I ever jump off anything?"

"Scared of heights," he says. "Of the color blue."

I'm instantly triggered.

"Hates loud noises but prefers them to silence." He moves right in front of me. "But the worst, the very worst, is when someone touches your ear, and you want to know why?"

I stumble back. My ears have always been sensitive to the point that even doctors couldn't check them.

"Because..." He takes a step toward me. "The ears can't forget what they hear and if what they hear is so painful and sensitive to the psyche, they bleed, they break, they mourn, over and over again, to the point of forcing the eyes and the brain to forget. Your ears are your savior, and yours have been doing it for a very long time. I think I might take them now. It's time. You've been given three, four isn't heard of, so let me take them."

"Take my ears," I repeat. "And wh-what would you do with them?"

"Use them, of course." He grins. "I would give them to her because, at the end of the day, you have to give a token in order to gain a favor, and she's been dying for your ears for a very long time, the way she wanted something else and got it." He looks behind me as if searching for something. "Sad that you have scars."

"What?"

"Hey!" Horus shouts from near the back door. "Who are you?"

The guy before me pales and then disappears like he was never there.

Horus jumps in front of me, grabbing me by the arms. "Are you okay?"

"Yeah." *No.* I nod. "That guy."

"Not a guy." Horus shakes his head. "That was a shadow. They work for the lower gods and goddesses in hopes of earning enough time to gain back their original place in the cosmos."

"A shadow?"

"Of the past. Your past. He wanted something from you."

"He said he wanted my ears." I feel dumb even saying it out loud; I'm shaking and trying not to burst into tears. "He said that, that hearing—"

"Shhh." Horus holds me against his chest. "Let's just go back to my place. I'll try to figure it out for you."

"Says the god." I joke. I have to.

He laughs. "Yes, says the god of the sky. I mean, I do know things."

"Can you know this one thing for me?" I look up into his blue eyes, still trembling over the encounter.

His breaths come faster, and his eyes hood; he lowers his mouth to mine and presses a gentle kiss against my lips. "My promise," he says, tasting me gently. "I'll figure it out for you."

"Why?" I can barely breathe he's squeezing me so tight, but he refuses to make eye contact like he knows something I don't, and he's afraid to tell me the bad news. I can't believe I'm actually clinging to him the way I am. I just know he's safety, he's protection, he's no longer the grumpy trainer—

though he still has his temper—he's security and promise. I just wish I knew why I feel this way and why every time he touches me, my lower back aches.

"Because we're connected, I think. Because I care. Because…" He shakes his head. "I wish I had more answers, logic, solid reasoning for holding the woman I'm supposed to be training behind the bar after a phantom decides to lure her away. Maybe because I'm a god. It's what I do."

"You kiss random strangers?"

"No." He smirks. "I haven't kissed anyone in a very long, long time."

I feel special in that moment. Needy. "Good reasons."

He nods his head. "The only reasons I have for you right now."

I grip his shirt. He wraps his arms around me. I don't know why, but I need to deepen the kiss. He does it before I can, his tongue brushes mine, and I'm suddenly lost in him. My hands dig into his hair, he groans, and then I'm lifted against him. It's all about us. I don't care about anything else.

"Later," he says between kisses. "I'll figure it out later."

"And now?" I ask.

"Now." He yanks me against him. "I want you."

THIRTEEN

思えば思わるる

Omoeba omowaruru

"When you care about (someone), you will be cared about."
Love and be loved. / Love is the reward of love.

~Japanese proverb

Horus

I'm out of control. Even as I say it in my head and own it, I can't stop it. I tug her into my apartment, thankful that it's Tarek's night to close.

I slam the door behind us. "Sorry."

"Why?" Her eyes are thoroughly unfocused. Something isn't right. I wave my hand in front of her face and drop it.

She's not present with me.

She's somewhere else.

I frown and gently pick her up into my arms. I kissed her, or she kissed me, whatever. There was something there. What happened? Where has she gone? I have no clue what's going on as I lay her down on the couch and wait. I've never experienced this urgency with a total stranger before; it's invigorating, even if it is terrifying. What did Timber say to me the day after I was stuck in this timeline? To live my life to the fullest? Is that what this feeling is? Living with weakness but relying on someone else even if it doesn't last forever?

She is nothing to me, and yet I feel a pull.

Is this the lust I've been watching over and over again at the club? The reason men and women get into fights, the reason they cry out for each other, hit each other, puke on the ground, or drink too much trying to get over someone? In all my years, I have never known that sort of pull, only that of the people worshipping the random women I slept with to pass the time and me.

My powers are weak, but I can at least see what she's seeing; maybe that will help me without having to go down into the Abyss to figure out what she actually is.

Maybe this will be enough to protect her in this lifetime.

I wave my hand over her face, then press my fingers against her temples.

She gasps, her chest rises hard, then falls. Her eyes close. Shit. I press harder and close my eyes, and then I wait.

"I will love you forever," she whispers. "No matter what."

The man sitting next to her has dark hair and familiar tattoos running down his arms; he flinches and then looks away. "Forever is different for so many people, just like futures."

"Then exist in mine." She grips his hand. She's so happy like she'll spend a lifetime with him.

"You're not human, and you belong to someone else." He slowly pulls his hand away from her. I feel the loss as if it's my own. "It's not meant to be."

A tear slides down her cheek. "So you'll marry her then?"

He stares straight ahead. "It's my destiny. Unless you want me to marry you, then kill you, which would be yours."

"And love? What about that?"

"Weakness." His voice cracks, and he turns to her finally. "You're my weakness, little fox."

She gasps like she can't believe what he's saying. "But we were together, we were one, and once a fox gives itself, it's forever!"

"For you." He stands. Shakes his head. "Not me. You never gave me your more prized possession."

My heart burns when he walks away. She stumbles back into the forest. Rain begins, a few drops at first, but it quickly becomes a deluge, as if the sky is weeping with her. She is drenched in seconds she crumbles down into a cave. "WHY!" She shouts.

She lies across the forest, years pass, and she meets someone else. I don't see his face, but he wraps her in his arms, he flirts with her, he stays with her, and he protects her fur from the rain.

I'm instantly jealous of him.

Of what he's experiencing as they talk deep into the night, as he shows her the stars and tells her that her destiny was never a puny human but greatness.

"I must go," he whispers weeks later. "But I'll come back. I'll always come back."

She waits in the rain for days, and then a voice sounds.

"A trade." The female voice coos over the wind.

I can't go further. As much as I want to, I can't.

I grip her hand, though, the way he didn't, and I hold it tight; I hold it until she finally opens her eyes; even though I'm in the present, not her past, I still hold her close. Who would dare leave her?

"Tell me," I whisper. "Tell me your darkness."

"Are you so pure you can consume it?" she asks right back.

"Are you so lost that you can't remember it?"

A tear slides down her cheek. "All I remember is sadness, rejection, and isolation."

I swipe the tear with my thumb. "Shall I find you then?"

"Is that a god thing?"

"It's a me thing." I offer a hopeful smile. "But only if you'll let me."

She's quiet, but on an exhale, she nods. "Then search."

I touch her temples again. I don't see anything bright or pretty. I see confusion, I see sadness, I see someone being blocked.

And then I see a trade.

The same trade I just witnessed her discussing in my dream, but later.

She gave something to get something.

But what?

It changed her; it forced her into lifetimes. I frown. She's so many things and yet still herself. She has to win. She has to!

I jerk my hands back. They're shaking; I couldn't stop them even if I wanted to. I've only ever seen this once in my entire existence.

"What?" She grabs me by the shoulders. "What? Why are you looking at me like that?"

"You," I whisper. "You have one lifetime left, and then you will cease to exist."

"What?"

"You traded your life. That's all I know. And if you trade one thing, you have to fix it by gaining something else of equal value." I shake my head. "I can't help you unless I know who it was you traded with."

Her head lowers. "I don't know. I remember nothing."

"Who would?" I ask mainly to myself, then remember Bannik, the Watcher of the sector she was in.

Why is it even tempting me?

I shove the thought away and pull her into my lap. "We'll figure it out."

"You're familiar."

I don't even realize I'm petting her head until I lower my hand. "I'm sorry that was really inappropriate—"

"Please don't stop," she sobs against my chest. "It's been an eternity since anyone petted me."

Is that a thing certain humans enjoy?

I hesitate, and then my hand comes down on her head, up and down; my palm caresses her head until she turns against me and rests her cheek against my chest. "It's nice being touched."

"How long has it been since anyone touched you?"

"I don't remember. But it never felt like this." She wraps her arms around me. "I've never felt safe, I don't think. Not until this moment." Her sigh reaches into me and whispers to my soul. "Will you keep me safe?"

I swallow the lump in my throat. I feel like I'm on the edge of a cliff ready to tumble down it, yet not ready at all for the consequences of my actions. "Always."

She burrows her face into my neck. "Thank you. I think I'll sleep now."

What the hell is going on? This is when having all my power would be extremely useful, and yet I'm powerless to see her future, to truly go into her past for longer than a few seconds, to taste her soul and feel her need.

"Okay." I cradle the back of her head in my palm and lay my cheek against hers as I murmur, "Sleep."

Minutes later, Tarek walks into the apartment, takes one look at her sleeping against me, and smirks. "Good night?"

"I'm confused," I whisper.

"An arrogant god confused? Best night ever." A knowing grin slides across his face, and he winks. "She's clearly connected to you... and not human. So figure it out, god. Our end might depend on her beginning."

"She's that important?"

His grin abruptly falls away. "What does your heart say?" he asks. "The same one slamming against your chest, telling you that this is different, important, not normal. Ask your heart and if you're still confused, ask your family at dinner. It's not like you can get out of it anyway, none of us can and the last time Timber did Cassius threatened to set his ass on fire with real fire from Hell. I've heard it's blue and that it's hotter than red, but what do I know?"

I almost curse.

He holds up his hands. "Hey, it's not like you don't have resources. When will you stop relying on only yourself? Maybe your big test is learning to share the burden you've always carried." One bushy eyebrow quirks upward. "Ever think about that?"

He's gone before I can answer.

I hate that he might be right.

Instead of arguing further, I tuck Kit against my chest and pull on a blanket, then try to get some sleep, wondering the whole time how I can help her, help my family, help myself... without getting lost again too.

FOURTEEN

以心伝心

ishindenshin

"Heart to heart."

~Japanese proverb

Kit

I sleep the best I've ever slept, or at least it feels that way, and I'm not even surprised when I wake up on Horus's couch. It seems to be my new normal. The last few nights, he hasn't let me sleep at my own apartment, and I can't be mad about that. I feel safer with him.

With him and Tarek.

I stretch my arms over my head or try to then realize something is against me, something that smells good and is heavy.

Horus is splayed over my body, his face literally resting on my belly button; he's so heavy I don't know what to do. If I push him down, then… well… *that's* not good. If I scare him, he might freak out, and at least one of us might get hurt. So I just clear my throat.

Lame.

"Ahem." I do it once. Twice. "Ahem."

It's just as bad as if I tapped him on the back or snapped my fingers and then cleared my throat.

Horus sighs, and his hands move to my hips; he grips them, and the sigh becomes a groan. I can't say I'm unresponsive as his fingers dig in. "So good," he moans.

I don't say yes out loud; I just think it.

Tiny electrical charges zap outward from where his hands hold on to my hips, radiating down my legs to my toes and upward over my ribs and to my neck and into my ears, setting the tips on fire. I cannot remain still and begin to writhe beneath him.

He's right… it's all *so* good…

"Stay still," he rasps.

If my entire life brought me to this moment, I might say that it was worth it to die young with the way his fingertips dig into my skin and then pull my hips down like he's slowly crawling up my body… He covers me, taking his weight on his elbows, and his mouth finds mine.

A bright spark nips my lips.

This is my destiny.

His mouth.

It's what I've been waiting for.

And it's so familiar.

It's mine.

A tear runs down my cheek.

He's always been mine.

What is this feeling?

Why is this man mine without me ever knowing him? We've never met, and yet I'm responding in a way that makes my heart ache so much I can barely stand it. I've never been the type of person to have a one-night stand, let alone just shack up with a guy who says he's a god, even though I've seen and felt proof. It's all so foreign, but at the same time right. It's right to be in his arms. My breaths come out too fast though, and I can't suck in more air.

I start to hyperventilate.

He pulls back, his expression still clouded with desire. "Kitsune?" But his eyes are gold. "Are you okay?"

Rain pours down around us in the forest while he smiles down at me, his eyes still etched in concern.

Who's Kitsune?

Not me.

I jerk back and fall onto the ground with a thud... then realize it was all just a dream. He's still passed out on the couch, and I'm on the cold hard floor, finally able to remember something that never really existed.

The same face.

The same memory.

Same past.

Same loneliness.

I wish people truly understood what it felt like to be lonely. Sure, I can be starving, thirsty, I can be depressed, and anxious, but to truly have no human connection at all. To walk through life without... I think I'd rather die. How funny; not even a self-proclaimed god can save me.

Figures.

I take a deep breath and stand, but I have no opportunity to step away before Horus's hand snakes out and grips my wrist. He lifts my arm to his face and sniffs, then locks eyes with me. "Kitsune."

"What did you say?"

He jumps to his feet. "I dreamt of you."

"What?"

His eyes fill with tears. "I know you. I had visions, dreams. You're... something important."

"You said that."

"You healed me," he whispers. "I was bleeding, and you fixed it. I was out of my element, out of my zone of protection. I was weak, and you... healed me."

"What are you talking about?" I ask.

He shakes his head. "How far do you think someone would go to save you?"

"What?"

"Wait for me," he says the words like they're so final. "Wait for me."

"Wait for what?"

"Retribution," he says. "I'm going to tell you who you are. I'm going to save us and repay the debt."

"What freaking debt?" I yell.

His smile is sad. "Once upon a time, a fox gave me her bead in order to heal me. I never forgot it. I gave it back, but I also never forgot her. But then she lost it again... I'm going to find it."

"A fox?" I ask. What do beads do, and why does that feel like I should know this story?

"A fox." He nods. "I finally know. And I know who to ask. Just wait for me and try not to piss off Tarek." He sighs. "A fox bead is the most precious thing to a fox with nine tails. It heals, it protects, it's what makes them divine."

I'm still thinking about how he's worried about pissing off Tarek. "Forget the bead. What about pissing off everyone else?" I'm clearly thinking about the immortals that I've tried not to think about.

"This isn't about them." He starts walking out of the room when a chill erupts around us.

Cassius opens the door like he just appeared out of thin air, which is strange, except Horus doesn't seem phased at all, as if he expected him to either try to stop him from making a choice or warn him that it would have consequences. "So you'll go, then?"

"Yup," Horus says, nodding eagerly. "Later this evening. I'm sorry I'll have to miss any future family dinners."

Cassius nods like he knew the answer all along. "I'll keep her safe. Just remember, your powers are limited, and you can't return if you don't win. And where you go, we cannot."

"She was mine once," he says low in his throat. "She was lost to me. So I'm going to win, no matter what."

"All right, god of the sky. All right," Cassius says. "Let the Creator be with you."

I lunge toward the door. It slams shut.

Cassius looks me up and down, then flicks his fingers, causing me to fall back onto the couch. "Sit, fox."

"Fox?" A frown tugs at my brow. I'm so confused I want to cry. "Where's the fox?"

He points to the couch, and my gaze follows his motion. In that moment, I nearly pass out as I notice nine fluffy furry tails resting against the sofa cushion and... attached to me. One of them twitches, and... I feel it! Only to have everything disappear into thin air. "Wh-what?"

" Nine-tailed fox. Kitsune. You're a kitsune and the only person able to figure out why you've been repressed..." He draws in a deep breath and then slowly releases it. "...rests in the Abyss. Pray that he's feeling generous. Pray your past love finds him and convinces him to help, or all will be lost. You have hours before he leaves, and even now, I sense the loss in you; I wonder why?" He shakes his head. "I cannot make choices for people, I can't make decisions, but all I'm allowed to see are all of the outcomes, depending on the path any being takes. Right now, the path is rocky, but it always has been between you two. For how could a fox ever fall for a god, and how could a god ever fall for a fox when he's on the other side of the world. He was hunting. He got injured, and while he could have self-healed after a few days, someone came and licked his wounds, binding themselves to him. I sometimes wonder if it was destiny or random. I guess it's not in my nature to ask now that things are moving forward. Just like walking into that bar for training. Just like being unable to sleep for fear of what the moon brings."

He's talking in riddles.

My fingers tremble as I reach for the tails; they fade in and out; they're a mixture of orange and white, so pretty I start to cry, but in an instant, they're gone.

As if they never existed in the first place.

Cassius stares me down with a grin. "It's Friday, isn't it?"

I'm still stuck on the tails, but I nod anyway, even as I will them to return. Not seeing them feels like being naked and exposed, without any sort of protection from the elements or from things that might want to hurt me.

"Immortal family dinner tonight." He starts pacing in front of me. "Are you doing okay?"

Loaded question. *I'm* still mourning the loss of tails I never knew I had but remember touching years ago. I frown. How many years?

Lifetimes? Past loves?

And now some random god I just met is hellbent on going to the Abyss, wherever that is, to find out how to rescue me? When did I ever ask for rescue? And why does it feel so familiar? Like he's done this countless times and in each of those times…

He lost.

I shake the dark thoughts from my head. "Yeah, I think my shift starts soon. Can I… um… maybe join you for dinner tonight since you just dropped a bomb on me and Horus just left muttering something crazy about the Abyss. And what is the Abyss anyway?" I hope my inquiry sounds casual, but clearly, it doesn't because Cassius doesn't answer. Maybe it's best that I don't know. Maybe the silence is the only response I'm going to get.

I touch my lips.

It burns where Horus kissed me, and I could have sworn it wasn't the first kiss between us.

I'm still overanalyzing everything when Tarek comes barreling out of the kitchen. "Geez, Horus is in a mood, I passed by him on the stairway, and he didn't even give me a high five, just grunted and said something about beads. Is he taking an art class we don't know about?"

Next to me, Cassius stiffens.

"Anyway…" Tarek tosses each of us a Red Bull. "Family dinner starts at midnight, don't be late. Please, for the love of gods, *come* to dinner. It's so boring without drama, and I think you guys will bring plenty of it. Oh, by the way, your tail's showing."

I gasp and look behind me.

He cackles. "Never letting that one go."

"Tail?" Cassius looks behind me.

"Stop staring at her ass." Tarek laughs. "Ah, sometimes I love my gifts; other times, I'm annoyed at how damn good I am at using them. Could have sworn you saw what I saw, but maybe it's different for angels with one percent evil in them."

Cassius glares. "Watch it."

"Cheers." Tarek lifts his Red Bull. "So I take it Horus has left the building in order to brood and prepare?"

"The Abyss." I frown again, wishing I understood more. "He said something about past lives, saving me, and the Abyss."

Tarek stops mid-drink and lowers his can, his eyes going unfocused. "Are you sure that's what he said?"

"I was here," Cassius adds. "I can only see the possibilities of his choice; I have no idea if he'll—"

"Make it," Tarek finishes. "Well, that kind of ruins family dinner before it even starts."

"What do you mean 'make it'?" I ask though I am absolutely certain I really don't want to know.

Tarek and Cassius share a look before the door to the apartment is shoved open, revealing Timber, looking ready to go to war. "Where is it?"

"Away," Cassius says. "To a place you cannot travel."

Timber's grin is downright sinister. He moves his head, and the overhead lighting flashes on his blond hair, even though it's shaved close to his head. His eyes go black. "Watch me, angel."

"Cease." Cassius holds up his hand. The entire room drops in temperature. "You may have been the lord of the underworld at one point, Timber, but right now, I have more power than you do, and the Creator has already made their choice. The best thing for you is to wish your brother good luck before he leaves and to help protect the reason he's leaving in the first place."

All eyes fall to me.

A chill washes over me, and I gulp.

Timber goes still, his eyes lock lifelessly on mine. His all-black suit suddenly seems to match the mood of the entire room and his teeth clench. "What if he doesn't survive?"

"Your guilt betrays you." Cassius crosses his arms. "He saved you, so you want to save him, but that's not your journey, Timber. That's your guilt. Go grab chicken for family dinner."

Timber shifts on both feet, staring down at the ground. His hands shake at his sides. Clearly, he doesn't want to move in any direction other than his brother, but after a minute during which no one speaks or even moves, he nods his head. "Chicken."

"Chicken," Cassius repeats. "Just focus on the chicken."

"This life," Timber says. "Not easy."

Cassius's lips form into a sad smile. "Life was never meant to be easy; it was meant to be long, filled with turmoil. Nothing lasts forever. There are only hellos and goodbyes. The point of life isn't to live forever, even as an immortal. It's to live for each small moment. Right now, yours just happens to involve chicken and a family dinner. Baby steps, god of the underworld, baby steps."

Timber squeezes his eyes shut. "Okay. Chicken it is."

Tarek grins between them. "Don't worry, you'll see, what should come true always does, and what happens isn't something you can prevent even if you want to, even if you had the power to."

I take a deep breath and look toward the bedroom where I stored my uniform. I realize that the only thing I can do right now, in all this confusion, is walk through that door, grab my uniform, put it on, and serve drinks. I can smile. I can live my life one second, one minute at a time, and pray that it's enough for when Horus, a man I never saw coming…

Descends into the Abyss.

All because he wants me to know myself.

He doesn't love me.

He doesn't need me.

He's a god.

And I suddenly realize that the gods of old that seemed so selfish are the exact opposite, because who am I that he would travel into darkness—just so I could feel the light?

FIFTEEN

惚れた病に薬なし

horeta yamai ni kusuri nashi

"There's no medicine for falling in love."

~Japanese proverb

Horus

Hours pass, hours of training her on the job. I need a few minutes to think so I go to the bar to set up for the customers. I need silence. And being too close to her was tempting. What if I just say that we don't return her past to her and what was lost. Memories we can make new, but parts of her that help her exist as she was created? I can't do that. As a god of the past, I would have been able to create her as new. I would be able to do with her what I did with my brother. But I used the last of my power to rebuild a soul on him, leaving her this soulless creature to walk the earth for maybe another fifty years if she's extremely lucky, only to die without a soul. A being, no matter how powerful, won't join the Creator if they have no soul, and she's already burned through what was given to her by living so many lifetimes in search… of what? Me?

Everything around us feels extremely mundane, human. But I still can't shake what I've seen with her and what I feel. Every single time I look at her, I don't see her the way I'm supposed to.

At times she's in the black T-shirt she wears for work, but other times she has on a Kimono in colors of bright white and brilliant orange, smiling over at me, serving customers only for the reality to slip back to the black shirt and denim shorts.

I shake my head and approach her. "Hey, you should probably take a break. You've been at it a few hours."

She stares up at me, her dark eyebrows arching like I'm about to get scolded. "I'm fine. I'm not the one who's going to Hell."

I freeze, then chase after her as she stomps off toward the bar. "Who said I was going to Hell?"

"I searched it on my phone." She grabs a tray and starts pulling empty glasses from tables; I'm surprised they don't break as she puts them on the tray. I don't reach for her though; I let her speak. She's angry. Anyone can see it. "I looked up the Abyss, it brought me to the book of Enoch. You know what that is?"

I swallow the lump in my throat over the brothers, who I know are still suffering because of their fall. Anyone else would laugh that she used the internet to find out the truth, but truth has a way of hiding in the most ridiculous places.

"It was never included in the Canon."

She's right. Enoch wasn't included for obvious reasons. It gave humans too much knowledge, too much access, and it was the final middle finger to the heavens for daring to say that the sons of man couldn't lay with women, that they weren't on the same level, that angels, while created, were nothing like humanity.

No. Humans were special.

Imagine being created as an angel, an immortal being for the heavens, only to be told this sniffling, sad, pathetic-looking creature…

Was the crown of creation.

Of course, a third of heaven was pissed.

And, of course, the church didn't want to include it in the Bible, and any other "religion" or sect, left it out as well.

All of them ignore the fact that, at one point, an angelic race of immortals were not just taken down by the darkness of narcissism; they were taken down by sadness and in their own minds.

Betrayal.

"Maybe you should rest," I suggest again a few hours later, grabbing her by the wrist and pulling her to the side. "Did you have lunch?"

Good subject change. Solid. Give me an award.

She jerks away from me and laughs softly. "I think I'll be okay." Her voice is quieter, subdued. I don't like it. "I'll just grab a protein bar before dinner. I have customers. I think I'm good, so you don't have to follow me anymore."

Is she already imagining me dead? Is this all for nothing? I take a step toward her, my arm reaching out. My fingertips touch her skin.

It's burning hot.

Her eyes flash at me, going bright blue before returning to the gorgeous chocolate color.

"Tell me," she whispers in my ear as we sit in the forest.
"You're pretty," I say quickly, holding her in my lap.
She rolls her eyes. "Not that. I didn't even finish!"

"So finish faster." I laugh. "Tell me what you need. What you want."

"You're not in your right time, Horus," she says sadly. "And yet you still visit me, despite knowing the eye of Ra watches, he always watches."

I look away from her and up to the sky. "He has bigger problems, and it's easy to skip through time and memories to find you. I'll always find you, ever since that first time. Wasn't that my promise when you gave it to me?"

She cuddles against my chest. "The only thing that allows you to travel through, the only thing that gives me hope."

"The most important thing in your existence, more than your soul. Your life, your meaning." I nod. "And now…" I part my lips as glowing red flicks of fire ignite on my tongue. "I give it back, just like I return it to you. I'll return. Ra said it was my destiny to be with you. Give me a day, and I'll come back and bring you with me. We can get married at the temple of Horus."

"Wow, thinking highly of yourself?"

"They worship me." I laugh. "And they'll worship you the same way, bring you dresses and food and gifts. It's everything you deserve. Nothing can go wrong at this point. My brother's been grumpy lately, and we're just about to join our family with the Greek Gods. An alliance like this has never happened in history. We'll be all-powerful, which means I can do whatever I want. And what I want… I lean down and press a kiss to her mouth. "…is this sly fox."

"Dumb bunny."

"Wrong timeline." I laugh. "But still cute."

She scrunches up her nose. "You promise you'll come back for me?"

"I could never forget you," I whisper, pressing another kiss to the corner of her mouth. "You're my Kitsune. I'll catch you any day; I do like hunting."

"That is how you found me."

"You should never have come near me or tried to save me and my wounds."

"You should never have come out of your space. I had no choice." I smile. "You're mine, you know that, right? My destiny?"

I don't look like my godlike self. I look more human, with tattoos of my heritage down the side of my arm, my hair's darker, not light, I'm existing as something other than myself, which is fine because I have to wait for her, and if I was full god, my father would see, and while I'm not afraid of my grandfather, Ra, my father has plans for rulings that alarm me, especially now that he's going to marry Kyra, the Greek goddess.

We have to align the immortal gods now that the worship has lessened, and I don't know why it makes me feel leery, but it does. In theory, it makes sense, but when has my father ever respected the Greek deities?

I shake the thought off and turn back toward Kit. "Together forever," I kiss her right temple. "Now, go hibernate. I'll be back before you know it."

She nods. "I'll dream of you."

"Please do." A grin breaks across my face, and my heart fills with even more emotion. "And when you're afraid of the darkness... look to the sky. I'll always be there."

"Good." She nods. "That's good."

I leave her.

"Watch where you're going!" a customer shouts as I collapse against the table and onto the beer-spilled floor.

Kit drops to her knees and starts rubbing her wet rag over my arms. "Are you okay?"

No. I'm not.

I was hers. She was mine.

And yet here we sit—in a bar.

I'm covered in sticky beer and who knows what else, and she has no idea the past we've had, and I have no idea how to fix it.

Well, I do. And despite my stated intentions, I have to admit I've been wary about actually following through with it, but now I know.

My future was broken, and so was hers.

In order to fix the future, remember the past.

I'll go.

I'll dive down deep into the darkness, allowing it to swallow my sky whole in hopes that, in the end, she feels the warmth of the sun again and that the moon yet again rises to guard us.

I'll go to the Abyss.

Even if it means my death.

She's dead on her feet. I can tell she's tired, exhausted really. It's not a full moon, but her face lacks color. And still, she pushes on.

I growl and stomp back over to the bar. Tarek's whistling to himself, then he starts singing to himself.

"Who is she?" I ask.

He looks up at me. "Who's she?"

"Kit. She's more than a fox. Something's going on, something I can't see more. She's tied to me in a way I can't explain. I feel things I shouldn't feel after only knowing her for a few days, and I think I know what I need to do; I just don't understand what's compelling me so hard to do it." I sigh. "I see memories, but then I doubt myself because I'm out of my own timeline. Are they hers, mine, both? I'll fight to save her, and yet I wonder why. It's all just so confusing."

He grins. "Not my journey, not my path, but thanks for asking. Oh also," he says with a snap of his fingers, "Timber said you hate ham. Are you good with turkey?"

I will kill everyone. "Turkey." I can barely get the word out.

"That's what I said, but then he was all like, oh chicken, but he like chickens because they used to sacrifice chickens to him, so it's like a favorite."

I remember a lot of chickens and feel actual trauma. "*NO* chickens!"

Tarek grins. "Good thing you have me then, right?"

"How do I help her?" Other than walking toward certain death.

He starts wiping the bar top vigorously. "You already know. It isn't a question of how. It's if."

"If?"

"Or maybe, will you?"

"And if I do?"

"So many possibilities. I mean, that's my only job, you know that, right? I see multiple possibilities, futures, lives. I'm not even sure at this point; I just know that working at this bar every day isn't going to give you the happy ending you deserve, god of the sky."

The entire building shakes for several seconds.

"See?" He cackles. "Your power burns to be set free, but you will never be fully yourself in this timeline unless you sacrifice. Don't you get it? Sacrifice means sacrifice. Giving up. You have to do whatever it takes to be your true self here. Selfless. Fucking storm the gates. Become who you were here, and you will be."

My memories jumble together. "I thought I was limited."

"Limits exist in timelines only if we allow it." He says it like it's so simple. "Anyway, I chose chicken, and we have to leave in like five minutes. I'll grab Kit."

That's how he leaves me, with a choice between family dinner at least for tonight or really going toward the Abyss in a sprint. I'm more frustrated than ever and terrified I won't be strong enough to make it back to her. Does he see something I don't? Is he trying to warn me to make a different choice?

My only goal is to return to her even if I'm not the same.

She has to know she is everything.

She's important.

She's mine. And always has been, even if she never knows it. I watch her laugh with customers. Sure, we kissed, and she feels something, but she has no clue. The past memories, the things we shared. I'm still trying to understand the fuzzy memories, but I know in my soul they're real even if she doesn't see it.

She has no idea, so I sit there, and I allow every memory that I can finally reach to pour through my brain.

Our first kiss in the forest.

Tag with the other foxes.

Telling each other stories. Decades and decades of stories.

Her head in my lap.

Me petting her head, running my fingers through her hair.

And then darkness. I can't see anything other than a dark prison, screaming, and hands. Massive hands reaching through bone and stone-filled bars.

I jerk back.

"Are you okay?" Kit comes up to me and smiles. "You looked terrified."

I want to say I am scared that even as a god, I'm limited right now, that I may not come back, and then I remember her kiss. I remember memories she has no idea even transpired.

I remember loving her so deeply.

My heart aches.

A fox, according to Cassius.

A fox? Really?

What could a mere shapeshifter give me to make me abandon everything in my world for her?

Part of me realizes I may not remember, not because I didn't experience it, but because I left my timeline, so maybe my past self did, and I'm just seeing pieces of visions of his memory which almost makes it even more sad.

He got time with this glorious creature.

I got memories.

"I'm fine." I force a smile. "Enjoy dinner tonight. I think I'll go get ready."

She grabs my hand. "You don't have to do this. I'm fine as I am."

I nod and meet her pleading gaze. "But I do. Because you aren't who you're supposed to be, and without an identity, you lose purpose. Without purpose, you aren't just roaming or lost—you're no longer human. You're nothing. You simply exist. You need more than that. I will give you that even if it costs me everything."

She shakes her head and looks down at her worn-out high tops. "Why would you do that? A god?"

"Why not?" I answer simply. "Is my job not to be benevolent and love? Are my job and my promise not worth anything? I said I would help you. Save you. Come back. And you said you'd save yourself. So maybe this gives us all a clue in how you, a small Kitsune, does exactly that."

"Or I die."

"Yeah, or you die."

"You're supposed to be encouraging."

I smile for real this time. "It's been a short time here on earth; I'm confused easily."

She rolls her eyes, showing a bit of plucky personality. "I'm done in five and Tarek can wait. Can we maybe have a drink before we go to dinner?"

"Yeah," I murmur as a wave of longing—something that unsettles me—washes over me. "Just a drink."

And a sad dinner after, my last.

A twinkle sparks in her eyes. "Did you want more?"

"Always." I decide to answer honestly.

She laughs, perhaps a little sadly, or perhaps that's my imagination. "You barely know me."

I don't return her laughter; just simply lift her chin with my thumb. "You have no idea… how long I have known you."

"So…" I break the silence as we drive toward Ethan's for dinner in one of Tarek's many SUVs. "First time eating with a vampire?"

Kit glares over at me. "That's not funny. I'm petrified, but thank you for that; super helpful."

We ended up taking too long with our last drink making

it, so I had to drive Kit while Tarek went ahead. It's killing me, being this close to her, smelling her, already missing something I don't know, but knowing if I fully had the ability to see her past, present, and future, it would probably destroy me.

"He doesn't bite…" I clear my throat. Though he *did* bite her, but only to try to find out more about her. Moving on. "I mean not a lot, from what I've seen. Then again, I'm new in this timeline, so—"

"Maybe stop talking now."

"Yup." I drum my fingers against the steering wheel of the Jeep until we finally pull into Ethan's compound, well technically, the Immortal Council's compound. Werewolves are guarding the gates, the doors, basically everything around us just in case, and I can feel the stars staring down intensely, almost like gravity is pushed harder here as we get out of the car and walk across the pavement. Any human walking onto this property would feel a giant sense of foreboding, like an invisible sign that says turn back.

I look up and smile. They're out in full force tonight.

The stars, they shine through you, pushing you into the ground, making it hard to walk, to breathe, especially when they watch and know that destinies are about to be changed, decisions made. They press down, they search, and they wait.

"Normal," I whisper to her and grab her hand. "The stars can't help but keep us grounded because our souls want to ascend, we want to go up, we want to join with creation, but it's not our time."

She grips my hand. "How do you know when it is?"

I hesitate, drawing in a deep breath. As a god, I know these things, but I've never spoken them out loud, the secrets of heaven. I stop walking and pull her into my arms. "Imagine this."

She relaxes against me. "Okay."

"Look up."

"I'm looking." Her head rests back against my chest. Is this perfection? I don't know; all I know is it feels right. Can I be selfish then? And steal more seconds and minutes, more moments from her so that if the worst happens, I can look back on this time, this sky, and say it was good enough? That I used those few seconds thoroughly.

I point up at the sky. "All of them, they sing, they sing day in and day out, they sing during the night. They tell stories of creation over and over again, and each time they sing over creation, they bring about destiny, but they can't interfere. Their job is to watch, to shine, to speak things into existence. That's why it's so important for humans to be careful what they say to the stars, for what they say… they believe."

She doesn't tense against me, but she does twist her head to gaze up at me. "So if I say I'm a star, I'm a star."

I laugh. "No, but if you say, I'm sad, I'm depressed, I'm a failure, if you say things like that, then yes, your mind will follow. Then your star will diminish, and when a star diminishes, it gets pulled toward the earth until it crashes against it. That's what we call a fallen star, one who has so much hope in its human that it is willing to sacrifice its life for that human. And if the human fails, the star does as well. That's why they watch. They each pick one—one human, one life, one source to breathe into. It's where dreams come from. Not the Creator, not your psyche. No, your dreams, they come from the stars, and your nightmares come from the death of your star as it crashes down to earth."

She reaches a hand up toward the sky. "So, god of the sky, the great and mighty Horus, how do I know my star?"

"You won't," I say, sadness filling my soul. "You can reach as high as you want, but your star no longer exists… it fell long ago. It saw you—" Visions hit me so fast my mind barely registers them, so hard I nearly pass out. "It fought for you. And in the end," I whisper, "your star, it died for you, died for your dreams, tried to fight your nightmares. Your star might one day be reborn, but today, your star is gone… all to save you."

I never thought to look to the stars, but now I know. It's as clear to me as the night sky, just another fragment of her past.

Her star sacrificed itself.

Why?

What is so important?

A star doesn't just fall.

It has to choose.

And once a star falls, there is no redemption, there is no savior, only hope that one day the person they sacrificed for sees the truth for what it is.

She's special. Not just to me but to others. I don't know how or why. I see nothing beyond the fact that she has a darkness where her star used to shine.

A single star.

I stare up at the sky.

I am god of the sky.

I know these things.

"…We protect, we save, we love…" The stars sing in unison. "We are one. We are one. We are one."

A star fell for this person next to me, the person with no memories, only tragedy, a person I want to kiss. A mere human, yet not.

I make a decision.

I will find her star.

I will save her.

Discover her secrets.

"What if it's you?" A voice whispers in the wind.

Me? Her star? I am the god of the skies, but… I'm not a star. I merely communicate with them; it would be completely impossible. But it does make me wonder, for someone who knew every name of every star at some point, which one was missing during her pasts that's still missing now?

In the end, wherever her star is, it will go back into the sky where it's meant to be, and Kit, she'll know her past; she'll be at peace, even if it means my death. Maybe that's the whole reason I'm here in this timeline, for this woman with tails, this person who can't sleep during a full moon, who has nightmares, who has known tragedies.

What greater purpose would my life hold than to help someone become who they are meant to be?

I think long and hard as the silence builds between us, becoming almost a tangible entity. Then inspiration strikes. "Let's go." I grab her hand, she doesn't see, but with my other hand, I wave off the stars and flick my wrist, allowing a dozen to soar across the sky like fireworks.

Show offs.

She gasps. "It's beautiful!"

"Yes," I say in finality, knowing I may not ever see the sky again. "It is."

SIXTEEN

因果応報
inga ouhou
"Bad causes, bad result"; "karma" or "what goes around comes around"
-Japanese proverb

Horus

I stay longer than I should, grateful that I made the decision to delay my quest to the Abyss until after dinner. I watch my friends—or family—talk around the dinner table over the stupid chicken they decided to grab, and I laugh when Kit smiles along with them like she's finally home.

It's pretty, her smile. I like it a lot, and I remember it well. I don't know how or why I keep seeing just bits and pieces or why I cannot seem to call to mind exactly who she is to me. I only recall sitting in a forest and promising her forever I had no business promising, even as a god.

She was so enticing, though, so perfectly imperfect. I don't know why, but I'm pretty sure she bit me the first time we met and then licked my wound clean and apologized for her manners.

I scolded her… I think.

She held her head down. Her tails swept the ground, the shame easy to see as dust clutters around the fur. But she doesn't know that what she does as a fox will always reflect in the stars, in the heavens.

I look up, and sure enough, she's swiped the stars to the left, to the right, and then rested, staring directly up at Orion's belt.

"It's a good story," I said, "of the warring angels."

"What?" she asks. "You aren't mad?"

"You're easy to love," I say simply. "And the skies, they change constantly. Sometimes it's an itch from a fox; other times, it's a breath of wonder from a human. A dozen lifetimes can cause the skies to move, but right now, you have Orion staring down at you. Angels and demons. I wonder what that means for your eternity… that they war for you."

"What?"

"Sleep." I press a kiss to her head. "Go to sleep, my precious fox. The thing about being a god—I worry for you, so you can rest. You rest, so you can wake up and find your destiny."

She crashed against the ground and then slowly crept up into my lap.

I remember feeling real warmth for the first time as I petted her head and watched the skies. My job had never felt so fulfilling.

The peaceful vision fades, but my sense of peace somehow remains.

I smile while she argues with Alex over the proper feeding of plants and animals, no clue where that actual argument came from, but he's clearly upset, he's not full god, but his eyes do go a complete white.

Everyone around the table laughs.

What a weird group.

Werewolves. Vampires. Sirens. Gods. Angels. Demons.

Life is never what you think.

I slowly excuse myself, scooting my chair back. It's loud. It's final. Everyone stops and looks over at me.

I smile, but it's sad. I can't meet my brother's eyes. I'll see too much in their eyes, loss, despair, hope, anger, sadness. I'll feel it all, and I might lose my nerve. Immortals are said to be good at shielding our emotions, but only from humans, not from each other. No, they may as well be screaming right now. I can feel it in the tension around the room, in the way the stars press down even onto that house, ready to shove me into the ground to keep me from taking the first step.

So I continue not to meet their eyes.

I choose not to meet hers.

I lower my head and bow, cross my arms, press my palms to my chest, and then extend them toward the sky. Slowly stardust appears around the room, falling in small tiny pieces of colorful ice around the table. My final blessing to my family and friends, to her, a piece of stardust, a piece of the sky.

A piece of me.

When I finally look up, it's to see Alex and Timber offering the same gesture back to me. I finally look into my brother's eyes and know what I see there. He is, after all, the god of the underworld. If I was braver, I'd walk up to him and say. "Anubis, tell me what you see. Weigh my soul."

And I'm positive he wouldn't do it unless I fought him, and even then, he'd reach into my chest and pull out a

"Maybe it's my turn to see those things." I grip him behind the neck and pull him in for a hug. "I'll be back before you know it."

His eyes fill with tears. "Okay."

They reflect nothing but darkness.

Mine reflect the light of the skies.

Opposites yet blood. Maybe I was brought to this timeline for this very purpose; who knows the true meaning of destiny?

"Okay." It feels like goodbye because a small part of me recognizes that it is. I don't want it to be over, but can I not celebrate that it happened? That I existed here, that I'll at least be able to save parts of a person that was, at one point, my North Star? I turn toward her sleeping form and press a kiss to her forehead. She mumbles in her sleep and reaches for my face.

"You promised," she whispers. "You promised you'd come back."

I swallow the lump in my throat and nod at Timber. I refuse to hug him again or tell him my regrets. I hope my eyes say enough just like his do, and I turn.

I turn toward my destiny.

I'll save her even if it means destroying myself. One life is never long enough when you don't know who you are or why you are, and she deserves to know at least that.

I promised.

And when a god makes a promise—that god is bound to it.

I follow Cassius out of the house, and we walk. It's nothing special. Gravel crunches beneath my feet as I walk behind him into the darkness. His massive form keeps flickering flame, one that knows it's about to be sacrificed, and I wouldn't make a different choice. I need answers, and the more I think about it, the more I realize this is something I should have done a long time ago. I learned how to sacrifice for others rather than expect them to offer themselves to me. Is this what happens when a god wakes up? When he realizes how selfish he has been? Is this love? And why do I keep asking the same question over and over again, what's love? It's like I'm desperate to find it and know the only way to do so—is to die for it.

Cassius stands, his multi-colored wings fan around him. His hair glows white, along with his eyes. His whisper is full of pain that I feel down to my bones. "I'll take you as far as I can."

"But wait!" Kit yells.

I wave my hand in front of her face. "Sleep."

Her eyes are filled with rage before they close. Then she collapses against Timber's chest.

He stares down at her and then up at me. "Come back alive, you stupid god."

"Please, it's just the Abyss," I tease.

He nods. "You know what gods face down there."

"Everything." My whisper becomes a resigned sigh. "But I was god of the skies. I've seen stars reborn, and I've watched the heavens celebrate every single time a life was born, every time a life dies and ascends. I've watched the horror. I've watched the glory. I've made sure the sun sets and rises. What could I possibly face in the Abyss that I haven't faced while watching humans suffer?"

Timber's sigh echoes mine. "There is so much more darkness in the deep than you know. The things I've seen—"

walking without looking back. One might think him a giant if they didn't know the truth.

An archangel walks before me.

Paves the way for me in the only way he knows how.

Once a sinner, now a saint.

I follow him, head held high, and I look at the stars.

They shine down at me, but their song isn't the same.

I wanted a celebration.

I'm given a eulogy.

Sadness drips from the heavens with a thickness that becomes fog surrounding us as we continue to walk.

"…god of the skies, god of the skies, the walk it isn't bright," they sing. "It's filled with danger, disaster, and despair, the darkness you cannot bear. God of the skies, fight for your life, fight for your light."

I ignore their tears even as a light rain starts to fall. And that rain isn't normal rain; it comes from the stars themselves, their tears, both sweet and bitter because the god of the skies will no longer be with them… at least for now.

"Take care of them?" I ask Cassius.

He stops in the middle of a field and waves his hand over it. The River Euphrates appears in front of me; it's dried up more than usual and has been since the prophecy of old.

You can almost see the Abyss or the gates to it.

"I shall look to your stars," Cassius whispers, lifting his gaze to them. "They're as much a part of me as they are of you, and if all else fails, my father's aware, and he's already watching."

I frown. "Sariel?"

"My father. Yes."

"I thought he ascended. That he died to give you his powers. To make you an archangel?"

Cassius smiles. "For a god, you know so little. Nothing, really." He points up at the North star. "He's there, watching, waiting. Years from now, he'll be an angel again, but for now, he watches. Was that not his original job, god of the sky? To watch over humanity? He has merely returned to his baser form. He watches. And while he watches. I wait."

"Patience." I look out toward the sad amount of flowing water. Really, at this point, it's maybe four feet deep in places, with patches of sticky mud in others and some places completely bare, the river bottom dry and cracked. But the Euphrates still flows.

And until it stops, there is still hope for humanity.

"Any advice?" I ask.

Cassius waves his hand over the water. It parts, allowing me to walk through toward the gates of the Abyss.

I almost laugh. "That's some Old Testament voodoo right there."

Cassius joins in the laughter. "It's merely the water allowing you to pass. I was thinking more along the lines of Moana."

"Ah, so you finally watched it."

He barks out a laugh. "I like the songs."

"Of course you do." I laugh again, a little surprised that it feels good. I see my breath in front of my face and stare down the gates. They aren't what you would typically think gloriously dark gates would look like.

It's mud.

Mud caked on mud and a small window I'll have to walk through after surviving the suffocation of the mud as it collapses onto me while I crawl in.

It isn't heaven.

It isn't pretty.

This is a prison.

Cassius doesn't follow me; I can no longer feel the presence of the heavens or the Creator. Everything is cold and dark. It's the dampness that seeps into the bones… into my soul. My all-seeing eye can no longer see beyond the prison cell of a window I have to crawl through. My eye has always been part of my power; the great eye of Horus is part of the sky just as much as Ra's eye is part of creation. It's what helps me see even in this timeline. It's the one thing nobody can take from me, a power I was created with. Something I can no longer rely on as I descend. I've never been without the true power of being a god of the sky.

My steps falter.

It isn't because I have no bravery in me. It's because I feel abandoned, and I know this is just the beginning. As a god, I've always had the power of the skies, my eyes, I've had the heavens. I've even owned hell, thanks to my brother.

But right now. I am in utter darkness.

The great Eye of Horus, for the first time in history—can no longer see.

SEVENTEEN

負けるが勝ち
makeru ga kachi
"To lose is to win."
-Japanese proverb

Kit

My world is different now.

I don't know how it happened or why, but I realize this when Horus finally leaves. It feels different and weird, yet oddly comforting because I know in my soul he will come back. He has to.

We finish eating, and I go outside. I look up to the sky and wonder which of the stars picked me; which one fell? I spread my arms wide, do a little dance, and then stutter step.

I used to do that in the rain.

I don't know how I remember.

I frown and look down at my skin, the stardust reflects the sky like water on my skin, like a Christmas lotion you buy at the store, but it feels warm.

"Stay safe, god of the sky," I murmur.

"A gift," a voice whispers. Stars shine down on me so bright I can barely breathe; I fall to my knees as visions appear in my mind.

"Safe from who?" Horus laughs and chases me through the forest. "You're going too slow."

"Foxes are never slow!" I yell over my shoulder only to run into something warm and complex.

Horus picks me up, twirls me in the air, and then presses me against the nearest tree. "See? Slow."

"Kiss me." My breathless words are part demand, part entreaty.

"Is that allowed? For the loser to get a gift?"

I laugh, and my heart swells. I feel like I'm floating off the ground. Things are happier with him; I've been so alone, so isolated. The Watcher has left his post, and I have nothing but these moments with Horus and a dark foreboding that something else is present in the forest, ready to devour. I thrust the apprehensive perception away.

"Just one?" I tease.

He's beautiful; his golden hair falls past his shoulders, and his blue eyes only see me. Full lips descend and capture mine in a tender kiss. I want more. I wrap my arms around his neck.

He gasps in my mouth. "You tempt me."

"Good." I nip at his neck with my teeth. "Allow it."

"Allowed." He groans as my tiny bites find their way down his neck. I tug at his blue tunic and toss it to the ground, leaving it dangling at his hips; his chest is gloriously naked, and the tattoo around his eye seems darker as an even darker constellation of tattoos appear across his chest and stomach.

"Where's mine?" I point at his chest.

He swallows slowly. "Shall I find it for you?"

"One day." I smile, knowing that it may not be there, my star, my constellation; we've been in darkness for a while. I don't want to talk about sad things. "But today, can I just have you?"

"Isn't it past your curfew?"

I smack him on the chest. "Are you my guardian then?"

He makes a face. "I'm not that old."

"And I'm young?"

"Younger than me." His eyebrows arch as he looks around me. "Nice ninth tail. So what then, you're a little over a thousand years old?"

"Mature for my age, don't you think?"

"So mature," he agrees and pulls me down into the grass. We tumble over and over until he's on top of me.

My heart wants to join the song of the heavens. For this godlike creature is mine. He's mine.

"I have never in my existence hated my duty to the world more than I do in this moment."

My breath catches. "Why?"

"Because I want all of your seconds. I want your minutes. Your hours. Your days. I covet them, and I don't know if I'll ever have enough time to earn them."

"And if I give them to you?"

"What is sacrifice when it's unequal?" He smiles down at me. "Let me take a few more minutes though, just a few before I have to leave again."

I nod and meet him for a kiss. He tears open my tunic and reaches for my breasts while his mouth latches onto mine. His lips are always so soft yet unyielding, his hands massive as they cover my body, touching, exploring like he's studying everything that makes me alive.

His hand slides between my thighs.

I almost kick at him in shock. Never has anyone dared such intimacy with me. I open my eyes wide, torn—should I push him away? Demand he stop? Do I want to call a halt to things?

His mouth is still moving against mine, and so is one hand. With his other hand, he laces our fingers together and holds my arm down in the grass. I've never felt sensations like this before. Explosions like stars being born out of the darkness build around me as he touches every sensitive part of me.

Is this love?

I buck against his hand. He answers by pinning me against the grass and kissing me harder, pushing his tongue past my lips and brushing it against mine. He flicks a finger, deeper, deeper, ever deeper, as stars shoot above us. And I swear they're inside me too, as I fall under his spell.

"You will always be mine, Kitsune. If you get lost—look to the stars."

So I do.

I look away from him and up to the stars while my body explodes around his hand, while I feel lust and love for the first time and know I've been changed, and when he kisses me again and tucks my tunic back around me, I know. Even if my star is gone, I'll be okay.

Because I have the sky.

I choke on a breath and fall to the grass, and look up. I'm back at the house. I hear laughter. My face is wet with tears.

I remember that moment.

The stars.

More promises.

Slowly, I rise to my feet. And I walk alone to the house,

realizing sadly that many times I've been with him—but I've also been without him, and this is just a repeat of those times.

I force a smile. And walk into the kitchen.

The girls are busy drinking wine, talking about kids and family things. Meanwhile, the guy who claims to love me, to know me, is going into a place where he no longer has anything.

And yet he left me a gift.

Stars don't just fall, do they? I gaze upward one last time before opening the door.

No, stars don't just fall; they soar across the sky, lighting it up like Christmas. I smile as we walk back into the giant mansion. Men are on either side of the door looking more FBI than paranormal. I ignore the fact that the door opens on its own without anyone touching it, only to close behind us with finality.

This is where I'll stay until Horus comes back.

Because he *will* come back.

I have to believe it.

The girls, the wives, whatever you want to call them, are all waiting for me in the kitchen. Genesis is making cookies. Hope is feeding Genesis's kids. Kyra, half-Greek Goddess that she is, is looking at me with pity.

Mason's wife is currently pouring wine like we're facing the apocalypse.

And I know. I just know they're doing everything in their power to make me feel better, but their looks aren't helping.

"It's going to be fine," Genesis finally says, washing her hands. "It always is."

Stephanie walks into the room. "Of course, it will be. Cassius says it will be, so it will. He's, um…" She tucks her dark hair behind her ears. "He's at the gates right now. Horus."

"Has he gone in?" I ask.

She shakes her head. "He has to go in blind; he can't use his powers. The Abyss pulls your essence. That's why the four unnamed haven't been able to escape." She draws in a long breath. "There is nothing there that can save you."

"So, how will he break free?" I ask.

"He isn't imprisoned," Kyra explains. "He's visiting, so now we just pray that he brought something worth exchanging."

I freeze. "What?"

"You can't leave without a sacrifice," Hope whispers softly. I can tell she wants to reach for my hand, to comfort me. Instead, she keeps her hands at her sides, but her eyes say it all. "You must sacrifice for information, but also in order to gain back what you've lost, he has to lose too."

I stumble into a chair. "Why? Why would he do that for me?"

Genesis speaks first, coming over to me and wrapping an arm around my shoulders. "Don't you see? How can't you? He's known you in past lives; he loves you more than you'll ever understand. How could he not? That should be what you're asking."

I shake my head. "I only remember fragments."

I leave out the sexy one I just saw, and even then, my chest clenches. Who am I to deserve that sort of sacrifice?

"Exactly just like him, he wants to know more, and he's willing to sacrifice everything for it. For you.," Stephanie says. "Why else would he go? You're not human, and you've been suffering, and for whatever reason, he thinks it's his fault, so let him help and know that in the end, all we have control over is waiting until the results happen, waiting until it's finished."

I squeeze my eyes shut. "Does it always have a happy ending?"

The room falls silent.

"Okay." I nod. I draw in a deep breath. "Okay."

"Ladies?" Timber waltzes into the room. "Okay, bad timing, but I thought we could watch a movie while we wait?"

"How long will it take?"

Cassius walks in past Timber, grabs a bottle of wine, and starts to open it. "It could be minutes; it could be an eternity. Pray it's minutes because if he's stuck longer…" He checks the clock. "…then that is his new existence."

"No longer god of the skies." Timber curses. "But god of the Abyss."

Genesis releases a long sigh. "I think we could have been a bit more encouraging with that speech, guys."

"Sorry," they mumble in unison just as Ethan walks in.

He glances around the room. "What did I miss?"

She waves him off. "Put on a movie."

"No more Disney!" Mason yells from somewhere in the house. "It makes me sad!"

Alex starts arguing with him about why it should be the Disney special because of Christmas, and chaos ensues.

One by one and two by two, the group starts smiling and laughing.

Tarek tosses a pillow off the sofa at Alex, striking him in the back of his head. When Alex picks up the soft projectile and heaves it back, it catches Kyra in the chest.

Kyra grabs a different pillow and hurls it at Tarek, who quickly steps back. The pillow arcs through the air and lands on the nearly empty bowl of mashed potatoes Hope is carrying into the kitchen. She squeals and dumps what's left in the bowl over Alex's head…

As the roughhousing continues, I slip away and walk over to the window. Leaning my head against the cool glass, I gaze up at the stars.

"Please make it, Horus," I whisper.

A hand clasps my shoulder. "If anyone can, it's him."

I glance over at Timber. "You look too normal to be the god of the underworld."

He barks out a laugh and then shifts into his godlike form, making me so freaked out I nearly pass out on the spot. His head is a black jackal with eyes fiercely yellow, fangs huge.

"I take it back," I finally say.

"Most do." In a blink, he's back to his normal self, and he winks. "Now, let's trust my brother and go drive Alex crazy with more Disney. His least favorite is Up because he cries. I may have already pressed play."

I smile. "You guys are weird."

"Nah, we're just family."

EIGHTEEN

極悪非道

gokuaku hidou
"Villainy" or "diabolical"
~Japanese proverb

Horus

I stare into the darkness. Wave after wave of sheer blackness rolls over.

"You dare cross the borders, god!" The voice sounds like it's in eternal pain; a moan and choking follow.

I close my eyes, and then I pull off my black T-shirt and rip pieces from it, wrapping them tightly around my eyes, accepting the darkness.

I toss the remains of my shirt to the ground, standing in front of the first of the unnamed. "I need safe passage to the Abyss. I have someone to speak to."

"Stupid god." The voice chuckles. I feel his icy presence everywhere as the wind picks up. "If we can't leave, what makes you think you can?"

"Well…" I cross my arms. "I never did anything wrong.

I never fell. So if you'd like to continue this conversation where I tell you why you're down here guarding as one of the four kings until the apocalypse comes, be my guest. I love telling stories, and you already know how yours ends…"

"STOP SPEAKING!" he thunders.

"Oh, I thought you wanted me to defend myself. Or my purpose. Which is it, puny angel?"

He laughs. "Puny? Would you, as a god, put only puny angels under chains for thousands of years? We are not *puny*. We are just as godlike as you."

"And yet nobody worships you. Nor knows your name. Here's a riddle, do you even know who you are?"

He goes quiet.

I take another step toward the window, feeling the mud with my hands as I drop to my knees. "I would never enter the Abyss unless I could give the first guard a gift. Do you want to know your name?"

"LIES!" he shouts, and the earth shakes with his horror, his terror, and I realize it isn't just random terror. It's his own fear bleeding out with every breath. He can't help it because, in the Abyss, that is all you are.

Fear.

You aren't exempt if you're powerful. Fear will always exist. He places his palms on the ground. "You don't know it! Nobody knows it! I am unknown!"

"I'll carry it for you, the sadness on your shoulders, of not knowing who you are, of being sad over the fact that your star fell long ago and when it fell, the heavens turned on you, they went dark, so you've lived in nothing but darkness, and when you live that long in darkness you forget who you are, you forget your light." I open my hands wide, palm up toward the muddy window I must enter. "Your name..."

He's finally still. "It is lost, god."

"It was never lost, and neither are you," I whisper and hold my hands toward the skies. I call on his stars, I call on the heavens. I use my eyes for the last time to gain entry. I pull down the veil of stars. I use them, and I see nothing but glory.

This angel.

This angel.

His despair.

His fall.

Was for his family.

It wasn't selfish.

He will be reborn. He will be set free.

"You are very good, Ashtaroth."

The ground moves beneath my knees, and the mountains moan.

"What did you call me?"

"Ashtaroth," I repeat it. "Ashtaroth is what you were called. It is your name, your identity. You've done things that should not have come to pass, but in the end, you've also served well the heavens. And we know the Creator forgives. Let it fall away like the mud. Let it die one last time."

A burning rapture encases my body until I can barely breathe as I lean toward the cold mud and grip the bars of the window I must cross through. And then nothingness hits me as I'm brought to my feet in an instant. A hand grabs my throat, lifting me into the air.

A tear slides down my cheek. Is it over before it ever began?

The darkness is pulled from my eyes.

I see light.

Such brilliant light that I can barely breathe. I have to bow. I need to bow. I can't, but my body recognizes what I am seeing and my spirit even more. I dare not look into its eyes.

"You," he whispers, "are the second," he says as he shoves me to the dirty ground, "to name me in over five thousand years."

"Who was the first?" I asked.

His smile is sad. "My brother, Bannik, before he descended to the Abyss."

"I'm searching for him."

"He searches for himself as well," Ashtaroth says cryptically. "Your journey will be short, god of the sky. You are a creation just like me, and your power is limited here, even more so in the darkness. How will the great eye see if it has only darkness?"

"Faith," I say. "Complete blind faith. I have nothing to lose, only a really pretty fox to whom I made a promise. I will save her. Even if that means sacrificing myself."

He nods and waves his hand at the small window. "You may enter."

The pieces of T-shirt, muddy and torn, wrap around my eyes again as I walk through.

"For her sake," come his last words, "I hope to see you again." The sound of the window closing hits me with an irrevocable click. I'm lost in utter darkness walking through mud. My symphony is screams from people lost in the Abyss.

From angels suffering their fall.

I'm thankful I can't see them as I keep walking.

"HORUS!" one shouts. "God of the sky! Save us!"

"Horus! We worship you!" another shouts.

I shake my head. "We do not ever worship the creation, only the Creator." But my soul twists with the irony because once I enjoyed the worship of humans, and now it feels like it's all to gain something, not to give.

"BUT YOU ARE A GOD!" shouts another.

I keep walking through mud and filth as people shout at me. As the fallen shout, I walk with my hands out until I feel something hard. Doors, maybe. The doors to the true Abyss, not the prison for lesser beings, but the one holding the remaining three fallen of the apocalypse, the ones who will one day bring about the end of the world.

The one guarded by Bannik as his punishment for falling.

I trail my fingers over the cold hard stone, and in Japanese it says, "The one who watched will watch."

I lean my forehead against the hard stone. "Bannik.," I whisper. "I need you."

The stone begins to shake while the rest of the prisoners scream. I know this is unheard of. I also know I may never see light again, but I press forward as the doors creak open.

I feel nothing but a frozen cemetery around me. I keep walking. My footsteps fall hard against the cold stone, I can feel them through my boots.

"Why are you here, god of the sky?" a sinister voice asks. "Why have you disturbed my brothers and me?"

I inhale and exhale, then smile. "You miss it, don't you?"

"What are you talking about?"

"The sky." I nod. "You miss it. I could show it to you if you want to trade?"

"What could we possibly trade?"

I wave my hand over my head. "I'll make you a sky."

"You'll make a sky in the darkness of the Abyss? For what?"

"Past lives. A Kitsune, one from your guarded area so long ago. I need her memories. I need her past lives. I need a way to set her free."

Bannik bursts out laughing, something warm fans across my face, suddenly, flames appear, and I can see. The remnants of the T-shirt disintegrate and drop to the ground in ash, and there he sits on a throne of ice.

His eyes are black. His hair falls in darkness with red and white pieces pulled through the front toward his eyes by his temples. His smile is so cruel I want to look away. "You want to set her free for you or for her?"

"Her," I say instantly. "And you're the only one who knows the folklore of the past lives. You are the last fallen—" I catch myself. "The last to see the memories and myths. I can't access it because I'm—"

"Out of your time, yes, it seems you aren't where you are supposed to be, god of the sky. In fact, you're so far out of your realm, I wonder how you're even alive."

"Love?" I offer. "Perseverance?"

"What will you sacrifice?" Bannik asks. "In order to gain these… things?"

The sound of moaning reaches a fever pitch as the rocks around me start to move and shake. Pieces of rubble bump against my feet. I frown down at the alabaster ground.

"What," he says again, "will you give or sacrifice?"

"To you?" I ask.

"I do not rule the Abyss, you stupid god." Bannik laughs. "I'm merely her voice, and she wants to know what you will give?"

"Who is she?"

A female voice starts laughing; it echoes through the walls. "I collect. I collected from your brother, and I'm very much looking forward to collecting from you."

"One sacrifice?"

"What do you hold most dear?" the same female voice asks.

I stare straight ahead. "I admit, it's always been my power. Since I don't have Kit here, I'll have to say that my most prized possession is the eye of Horus."

"Idiot." Bannik spits onto the ground. "You'd give up what affords you the most power? Why? Why would you do that?"

"Shut up!" the female voice yells. "Shut up!"

"WHY!" Bannik jumps to his feet and starts pounding his bare chest. His movement allows me to notice that his leather pants are in tatters; he doesn't even have shoes on. I can hear the moans from his brothers. And yet I stare him down and wonder where it all went wrong. How the greatest of Heaven decided they would at one point just… give up.

"Why?" I ask. "Why did you fall?"

"Why?" he repeats, "did you descend to the depths of the fallen?"

"Love," I answer simply.

He nods his head, smile sad. "Is that not why we do what we do? It's either love or power. Every single time."

"Power for you?"

"Love," he rasps. "Not the kind you are experiencing."

His words confuse me. I'm still frowning when the female voice shouts, "MAKE YOUR CHOICE!"

"My eye," I say. "I give you the Eye of Horus."

"I wouldn't," Bannik warns. "She collects power. She'll use it—"

He falls to his knees in agony, screaming until his voice is hoarse, but even in suffering, he reaches for me and shakes his head as if to say *no, don't do it; it's not worth it.*

I wonder more about his story, this fallen angel.

He flips onto his stomach and digs his hands into the stone beneath him. Blood runs down his fingertips.

His back is covered in scars.

And where his scars are, I see two slants of protruding wings. I know what will happen next, they will grow, and every time they get big enough, they will get cut as a reminder that he's no longer an angel.

He is fallen.

He no longer watches.

He waits.

And his wounds will never heal in this place.

Bannik looks over his shoulder at me; his eyes go from black to blue as if he has a moment of clarity. He reaches for me. "She is a nine-tailed fox, and she is your destiny. But I cannot see beyond the betrayal. The forest. And what she gave. You wanted to save her. But she beat you to it, and she lost something valuable to you both, causing you to not meet until now."

I exhale. "Thank you, Watcher."

Bannik's eyes widen. "I am no longer a Watcher."

"You are what you believe you are," I say simply. "Just because you are in darkness does not mean you cannot see light."

I use the last of my power then, the last of my light.

I use my star.

The star of Horus, just as valuable as my eye, and I show him what he hasn't seen for too many years to count.

Stars being reborn.

His ability to be better.

To repent.

It's the last piece of light I have, and I give it to my enemy. The enemy of the immortals, of the Creator, the fallen.

But what good is light if you don't use it on the darkness?

I smile as I fall to the ground.

"You owe me your eye!" the female voice says. "I'll save her. I'll save her if you give me your eye, the great Eye of Horus."

"Sacrifice." I reach toward my face in utter darkness and press a fingertip to my eye, and smile. "Doesn't count unless it costs everything you have. Take my eye, witch, and let me sleep."

"Gods do not sleep in the Abyss; they toil." She cackles. "What will you do when you can no longer see, Horus?"

"We don't need eyes to see," I shoot back. "Take it before I leave you."

Searing pain stabs me in the chest, rising up toward my chin, then finally my eyes. I've never understood what it felt like to have something taken from you, almost like your soul leaving your body.

Just like Bannik's wings have left him.

My eyes have left me.

I smile the entire time. I smile through the pain.

She laughs.

But who will be laughing in the end? I have to believe justice will prevail and that the immortals back on the earth plane will win.

Otherwise, why would I choose to lose?

"Kitsune," I whisper. "She's soft."

Bannik laughs. "You're stuck here now, you know that, right? She won't let you go; you have no more favors or sacrifices to make in order to leave. You're an idiot."

"And you're brilliant?" I counter. "You've been down here too long."

"No." He stumbles to his feet and falls against his throne. "I'm trapped here not because I want to be but you chose this existence, so who's the idiot?"

"Still you. You tried to bring down the immortals, and what was it? Combine demon, and angelic blood, then imprison all your fallen brothers?"

He growls. "I had reasons."

"I'm curious…" I'm so blind it's strange, but I look toward where I think his body is. "What could possibly be the reason for that sort of sacrifice, Bannik?"

He's quiet for a long time. I see nothing. He finally answers in a low voice. "I wanted to redeem my brother."

I'm stunned stupid. "Sariel? Your brother? Cassius's father?"

"You need power to go against Heaven, and Sariel fell like the rest of us, but he never deserved to be punished because of whom he loved. I'll admit it became a thorn, a sickness in my soul. It became an obsession, and in the end, it was about me about powerful because of being so blind, but you know what's so satisfying about seeing no light?"

"I'm sure you'll tell me."

"You can only see your own darkness. You reflect. You watch over and over again, and you realize that in the darkness, the light isn't absent, it will always pierce through.

The sadness of that reality is that even if it does, a punishment is still a punishment."

"Misguided love."

"Such a bitch." Bannik laughs. "I've been very lonely. I'm glad it's you, Horus." He breathes deeply. "How is Cassius?"

"Alive. An archangel. A pain in everyone's ass."

"As he should be." He falls quiet. The darkness still carries moans, though, from prisoners. "And Sariel?"

"He shines." I smile to myself. "You should see him shine, Bannik."

" Can you explain it to me?"

"I can." A tear runs down my cheek. It's so dark. Shit, it's so dark in there. It's so empty. Isolated. I'm without my brother. I'm without Kit. My eye. I am lost, and yet, I know I need to focus on the memories, the light. "If you look up through the darkness, you'll see a very bright star, the North Star. He watches, he sees all, and right now, he's even watching us. You may not feel him, but you'll know your brother is here; he can't help himself."

Bannik laughs. "He's always been very intrusive."

I nod, hold my hands, and speak to the stars and the creators. I pray for the first time to the heavens in a very long time. I pray not for myself but for the fallen next to me. I've already saved the girl I loved. What was once taken from her will be returned now that the goddess of this Abyss has my eye; she'll have her memories, and she'll have her identity even if she doesn't have her star.

She'll wake up and remember everything. Memories will assault her, and she'll realize how special she is and will always be to me and the world. She'll be immortal; she'll have everything because of my sacrifice. Is that not how this works? An eye for an eye? An eye for what she sacrificed, and now, she will join the Immortal Council. She'll be able to live and laugh and love.

I hate the last one.

If I can't get back, she'll eventually love another. I hate them already.

I have nothing left. I ask. I pray.

"Creator."

It's all I have on my lips as darkness descends, and then I smile. I smile because I see her. I see us laughing and kissing.

"I love you more than anything." I press my mouth against hers. "My little fox."

"I'm a grown fox!" She shoves me.

I grip her hands and twirl her around and around. "My grown fox, then."

Her eyes fall. "And if I want foxes?"

"You'll have everything, am I not a god?" I joke.

She twirls again in my arms and leans her back against my chest. "No matter what, I just want you. Which lifetime is this?"

The heaviness in my chest intensifies. "It's your second. You make it through one more lifetime as a human, and you can become immortal. You can become mine."

"Stupid folklore."

"Accurate folklore." I chuckle. "Every mythology has its origin, and yours is that you have to make it through three lifetimes as a human after jumping into the Abyss… you'll make it, though, I know it. We only have one more."

"And I'll know you? And visit you?" she asks.

I lie. "Of course. Isn't that how it works?"

It's not.

If she doesn't find me.

If I don't find her.

There will be no immortality. Or happy ending. Only her alone, isolated in a human world she doesn't belong in.

She'll be cold. Afraid. Alone. Terrified of the night. Of the full moon. Terrified that if she sleeps, everything will be finally stolen from her—including her bead.

The nightmare jerks me awake, and I realize I'm still in the darkness. I sense Bannik. "So this is our new future?"

"Yup." He sighs long and hard. "Should have kept your eye and left when you could."

"It's not so bad."

"Give yourself a thousand years, and you'll change your mind."

I shrug and sit up. "Things, they always happen for a reason."

He snorts. "What a horrible reason, brother, what a horrible reason."

We sit in darkness.

In silence.

I'm okay, though. I tell myself that at least she knows our past now; she knows why I fought for her.

I'm okay.

I hope she is too.

The others will help her. While nobody can rescue us, she at least has them. I find satisfaction in that and lay back down, staring up into the darkness, wishing I could see just one more star again.

Bannik makes a choking noise in his throat and then cries out. "They're cutting again."

"What?" I sit up.

I can't see him.

"My wings," he chokes out, his voice gurgling low in his throat. "It burns, it burns so bad. Tell me." He cries out harder. Screams erupt from his mouth. "Tell me a story."

"Second chances," is all I can say. "They always happen when we're in the darkness. So embrace that. Let them tear you apart. What can they do to a Watcher of the Abyss? A king? Nothing but pain. Embrace it. I'll be here the whole time."

"I've been so alone." He sobs. "So alone."

"No longer," I whisper, "will you be alone."

"No." A booming voice sounds. "He won't."

The earth beneath me shakes and shatters into tiny little pieces of clay, getting thrown against the walls of the cave. Light illuminates around us, exploding in what looks like an actual sun. It nearly overwhelms my remaining eye.

"S-Sariel?" Bannik holds his hands against his face, his fingertips allowing him to peek through. "What are you doing? You're a star! You have a purpose, a plan. You have—"

"Silence." His hair's red and white pulled back into a ponytail, and he's wearing nothing but low-slung black joggers as if he stole them from some random person before coming down here. "I'm here to make a sacrifice, he announces with finality.

"What?" Bannik and I ask in unison.

The feminine voice laughs. "Oh? And what could you possibly give me, oh angel of the stars?"

Silence, and then, "Myself."

NINETEEN

一刀両断
ittouryoudan
"One stroke, two halves."

-Japanese proverb

Kit

I see my past.

My future.

I'm in the present.

I'm sitting at the table holding a freshly baked sugar cookie, and all I keep thinking is, "I gave him my bead. It's all I have left."

Foxes have beads, what Horus's eye means to him, my bead means to me.

"What?" Hope nudges me. "Are you okay? You keep saying bead over and over again, and listen, I'm not upset about arts and crafts, but it's getting freaky when you start rocking back and forth." She takes a huge sip of wine. As she sets the glass down, her eyes widen. "Oh wait, is this like a code word for something else? I see how you look at Horus;

hell, everyone looks at him that way with his giant muscles and—" Alex kicks her under the table. "Babe, yours are way bigger, swear."

Alex grunts and stares me down, then her. "Why do you keep saying bead?"

"Bead?" I repeat. "Um, I think I lost it? I don't know, but these memories keep hitting me, and it's weird. What's a bead to a fox? Truly? I mean, I know it's important, like Horus's eye is to him, like your wings are to you." I point to Cassius. "But, if I sacrifice it, will it be enough?"

Cassius drops his fork, leaving half his peach pie, and stands. "So he did it."

"What?" I jump to my feet. "Horus did what? What did he do?"

Cassius stares me down, then the rest of the table, and then back to me. "Do you taste it yet?"

I'm so confused. "The dessert?"

"The bead."

Okay, these people are seriously crazy, even for immortals. "No, I don't taste a bead, and what do beads even taste like? And why would I be tasting one?"

"Fox," Alex says under his breath. "Nine-tailed fox from Japan. A Kitsune." He nods and stands. "She won't taste it until she sees him. They're connected, so even if he did succeed, she'll still be trapped."

"Trapped where?" I ask. Trapped doesn't sound good. It sounds terrifying.

Genesis sighs and looks at Ethan and Mason. "Should we figure out a way to go down and grab him? Would that help?"

"Help Horus?" I'm confused. If he did it, why isn't he back? "Why does he need help? Is he okay?"

Cassius slams his hands against the table and crumples to the floor. "Nooooooo!"

"Cassius!" Stephanie's at his side in an instant. "What's wrong?"

"Father." Cassius chokes. "Why? Why?"

Frost appears across the table where we've been eating.

And as a chilly wind presses through the room, we all look down and see on the table, etched through the frost: *"I will sacrifice and save until I can no longer. Be well, my son."*

Cassius looks away, and just like it appeared, the icy frost is gone.

And we're at the table with various sweets before us.

I'm traumatized.

Horus is gone.

And someone was just lost to Cassius. When will we get answers, and why does it feel like all is lost? It's so unsettling that I want to run and hide myself away.

Cassius jumps to his feet and leaves the room like the fires of hell are after him.

"Leave him," Stephanie whispers and grabs a bottle of wine. "Let's just continue with our meeting; he'll be back when he's ready."

Ready for what?

Is it always like this?

I grab my chair with shaky hands.

Minutes later, Cassius is back, and he looks oddly... happy. His eyes are shining blue, and even weirder, he grabs a glass of wine and then starts eating the leftover chicken still sitting mid-table.

Nobody seems to care.

I reach for my water, ready to ask him what just happened,

when the sound of the front door opening goes off like a bomb in the house.

He puts his wine down and leans back in his chair, an amused expression on his face.

I don't think anyone could have prepared for our visitors.

TWENTY

九死一生
kyuushin iishou
"Nine deaths, one life" or "near-death experience"
-Japanese proverb

Horus

"NO!" Bannik and I shout in unison.

"Interesting." She laughs, and suddenly I can see shapes in front of me. It's enough to see Sariel, he illuminates everything in this sick cave of darkness, but what he illuminates, I wish I could forget.

She has snakes wrapped tightly around her throat like a necklace. They dangle from her hair, falling down to her waist. Her eyes are black, her lips blue. "Hello, pretty little god of the sky."

I take a step back.

Bannik grabs me by the wrist and stands in front of me. He's so weak, one hit from her and I wonder if he would survive it, or if his hell is just perpetual pain. Can he even die? "Say your peace and leave, witch."

"Witch?" She pouts and crosses her arms, making her golden bracelets slam against each other. "A witch? I'm merely a fallen goddess that needs to be fed…" She peers around Bannik. "And this one seems delicious enough to eat… I told you I would come for you."

I take a deep breath. "Do your worst; I'm here for an eternity anyway."

"You think so?" She looks to Sariel and growls, her teeth clicking against each other. "This one might just free you by being… benevolent. I hate the angels that fall and fall again only to rise. I despise them." She eyes Bannik up and down. "But you, your life will always be mine. There are some who fall too deep, isn't that right?"

Bannik shakes at my side and continues to shove me behind him. "Yes."

"Good angel." She winks her black eye at him and stares at Sariel, tapping her mouth with her golden tipped finger. She's in a golden gown that falls from her shoulders like a cape. It would be pretty if it wasn't on a monster. "What will you sacrifice?"

"Myself."

"You said that, but you see, that's a trade where you give me you, and I give you one thing, and you seem to have two things here, so… you're going to have to make a choice."

Sariel actually smiles. He looks younger, his hair has gone from red and white to jet black now, and it shines like the sky that holds the stars. His eyes are bright blue. "You've been down here too long."

Her smile falters. "Well, that's no fun; you're just insulting me when we both know how this is going to end. You'll sacrifice yourself blah blah blah, and then you'll set one of these immortals free, and the other will, of course, become even more bitter, and surprise! I have more to feed off of!"

"Watch," Sariel whispers.

She frowns. "Watch what? Is there a hidden camera or—"

"Watch," he repeats.

Bannik's hand falls from my wrist, he starts walking toward Sariel, but I grab him. I don't know why. It's instinct. I grab him and pull him back.

Sariel smiles. "Watch."

"Shut up!" she yells. "Shut up! What is this?"

Sariel laughs. "Apophis, of course, you know what will happen to you, don't you? Once I sacrifice?"

"Apophis?" I whisper. The absence of light itself. She is darkness in my realm; she is Medusa in others. No matter what, she is the opposite of me.

The exact opposite.

I freeze. I can barely breathe.

Ra has battled for centuries with this goddess, and now she has my eye, the all-seeing Eye of Horus.

Bannik reaches for me again. This time, he's holding me back. He shakes his head.

"The thing is…" Sariel smiles sadly at us and starts to slowly walk toward Apophis. "You always need a prize to keep, am I right? Darkness can't survive alone. Isn't that how fear works? It must have a companion." He grins. "I live to serve my brothers." He nods to Bannik. "All of them." His eyes fall to me. I'm blind in my left eye, but my right sees him just fine. Even if I no longer have the same power, I see his.

He rolls his wrists. "Technically, I'm a fallen star. Take me, let them go, and I'll leave you what you've wanted for an eternity."

"What's that?" she shouts.

He reaches his hand out and touches her face. "Dear child… the only thing you can never have."

A red tear slides down her cheek. "I have everything!"

Sariel flicks his wrist, and I'm suddenly getting thrust backward with Bannik. "Child, you want what everyone wants."

"And what's that?" she repeats.

"Hope." He nods slowly. "And just one small flicker…" He snaps his fingers. "…of light."

Her eyes go from black to white as she watches the flame on his fingertips, and suddenly Bannik and I are tumbling backward until we hit the mud again. The window is just ahead.

"Come!" Ashtaroth yells. "NOW!"

Bannik stumbles backward in what I think is shock.

"NOW!" Ashtaroth yells again. "Seventeen stars have already fallen. This isn't good. They'll see, they'll know. You have to go!"

I have no time to argue; neither does Bannik.

We go from being in a dark prison to being shoved out onto the riverbed again. I choke out mud and darkness and turn on my side.

Bannik is on his hands and knees. He doesn't move. He stares down at the ground, and after a few minutes of silence, he finally looks up to the stars and lifts his shaky hands.

They tremble as he reaches for the stars.

I assume he's going to get sent back to the Abyss, but instead, I hear singing. "Return, return, one life is never long enough, king of the abyss. Be reborn, be reborn." His body trembles harder.

And one by one, nine stars crash to the earth around us, turning into water, crashing against the gates of the Abyss.

I stand on shaky feet.

Bannik does the same.

One star remains close to us.

I have no words.

I have only the air in my lungs.

I inhale.

I exhale.

"The morning star," Bannik whispers.

It doesn't crash against us; it doesn't sacrifice. It simply moves past us and through the gate, and I know... this will not end here.

"The morning star has descended," Bannik whispers, "to the Abyss."

"Good thing Sariel is there."

"They will battle."

"We will win," I say. "And sometimes, it's best to fight evil with evil. Apophis won't be happy with competition."

"And Sariel?" he asks. "What of him? What of my brother?"

I look to the sky with my one good eye. "Honestly? I have no idea. But I know he did it for a reason."

"And what of your fox?"

I shrug. "She has her memories now that I've traded my eye, she may love me or hate me. Who really knows?"

"Humans."

"I'm a god."

"Not in this realm. You're worse than a human." He dusts himself off and stares down at his hands again. They're dirty, caked with years of muck and filth. He has no clue where to go, or what to do.

I shove him toward the forest. "Let's go."

"I'm your prisoner now?"

"Yes." I roll my eyes. "That's why I'm helping you. Now, let's go. You have some people to apologize to."

I swear he pales even more, though he just keeps walking. Once we are at the edge of the river, I wave my hand and we're suddenly on the outskirts of the forest.

We walk toward the house.

I hear laughter.

They're eating still.

Time passes differently, doesn't it?

He stares at the house.

He wants to walk away. I can feel it.

After all, what good is the fallen?

He shakes his head and turns around just as the sound of wings fills the air. I look up. Cassius descends. His purple wings are razor-sharp and pointed toward Bannik. Cassius hits the ground with a thud and glares first at Bannik and then at me.

I expect war.

Instead, Cassius just sighs. "Don't eat all the ham; it's my favorite."

He walks past us and dusts his jeans off.

Bannik's eyes widen.

I shrug and start walking past our werewolf guards. "Come on, the food will get cold."

I know he'll follow.

I open the door. I take off my shoes and inhale the smell of food, roasted meat, and side dishes and the sweetness of baked goods.

It's at least one minute before Bannik's footsteps follow.

I keep walking.

He keeps following.

And then we're in the dining room. Everyone is gathered around the table with various desserts and wine. A well-picked-over platter of ham rests in the center of the table next to some leftover dinner rolls, obviously all that remains of dinner.

All talking stops.

It's Mason who jumps to his feet and yells, "YOU'RE HOME!"

TWENTY-ONE

馬鹿は死ななきゃ治らない
baka wa shinanakya naoranai
"An idiot can't be cured of idiocy unless they die."
~Japanese proverb

Horus

Everyone is silent except Mason. His eyes brim with tears, and I wonder how long he's waited to see Bannik again, a brother that his angelic part used to fight for, fight with.

Fallen into the depths of darkness, never to be seen or heard from since being bound to the Abyss a few years ago by the very people at this table for attempting something forbidden.

But things are different now. That's how change works, and while I wasn't here in this timeline when Bannik was punished, I know.

Bannik stumbles backward, colliding with the wall. Pictures crash to the tile floor, and glass flies everywhere.

Clearly, he's in shock, and I know it's not because he's never seen these people or tried to kill them multiple times.

It's because he sees his—

"Brother?" Bannik chokes out the word. "But how?"

"Funny story." Alex chooses the wrong moment to speak, but what else is new? "So he's a werewolf king, blah, blah, and since I defeated you, like, two years ago, I'm gonna spare you the hard details. Besides, you made me go full god, which was really freaking exhausting." He flips his hair. "Anyway… Mason, our werewolf friend here, has the blood of your fallen watchers in him. He's technically both. I mean, the logistics get weird, and we don't need to deep dive down into his story. Just know he's a werewolf with the blood of one of your brothers who was basically redeemed. Apparently, the Creator likes to get… er, um… creative. Yay, more wine? Anyone? Bueller?"

"Who the hell is Bueller?" I ask.

"Shhhh, let the grownups talk." Alex winks. "So Bannik, it's been a hot minute. You've looked… better. Need a little sit-down time or—"

"What the ever-loving hell is going on in—" Timber shouts, takes one look at Bannik. "I go to the bathroom for two minutes, and now we have a fallen angel, an archenemy just… dining with us?"

I shrug. I've got nothing.

Timber wrinkles his nose as he runs a critical eye over first me, then Bannik. "And dressed in your finest clothing, I see."

I don't even want to know how horrible we look, but I don't have to wait long for a fix. I have little to no power left, so I can't snap my fingers and make it better. I look to Timber. He sighs again and moves his hand under the table, a gentle tap of his pinky against his thigh twice, and suddenly I feel clean.

In the blink of an eye, we're both sparkling clean and attired in jeans and black T-shirts.

I grab a glass of wine and pull out a chair next to Kit.

She opens her mouth.

I shake my head.

She reaches for my hand and holds it. For now, it's enough. Romance and a show. Great!

Timber starts to growl.

I kick out a free chair. "Simmer it down, Anubis."

Timber gasps. "You only ever call me by my real name when you're pissed or annoyed!"

"Guilty." I sigh, my irritation. "Now sit."

"Anubis?" Bannik asks, looking between us. "He's Anubis?"

Cassius scoots his chair toward the table, making a painfully loud noise against the floor. Does he know how to actually get up quietly?

"He's clueless," Alex mutters.

"So dumb for being so smart," Timber grumbles, curling his lip in a silent snarl.

Cassius ignores all the comments and points to the chair. "Well?" His eyes focus in on Bannik in a way that's slightly terrifying. "Aren't you going to sit?"

Bannik's mouth opens, closes, then opens again.

"He's making fish faces. Is he even breathing?" Alex asks.

I can't stop the smile from forming on my face. "Those are chairs; they scared me too when I first got here. You sit in them."

Bannik scowls at me. "I know what a damn chair is, stupid sky god."

"I forgot how charming he is." Alex snorts into his wine.

"Do you think all that time in the Abyss made him a better person or worse? Shall we take bets?"

"How long has it been?" Bannik slowly pulls out a chair and sits right next to Kit. Why is she reaching for his hand?

Rage fills me when her hand fully slips from mine, and then she places a hand on his thigh.

He immediately calms, his eyes search hers, turning a bright white. He slams a hand onto the table.

"Mere years? Surely it's been longer than that idiot says." He's pointing at Alex with one hand and holding hers in the other.

What the hell is going on?

It's like neither of them even realize they're holding hands, and yet they do; it's natural, like she's found one who... watches.

I frown.

"Time passes differently in the Euphrates riverbed, Bannik." Cassius slides a glass of wine toward him. "So now you just decide what you will do with the gift of time you've been given and the second chance you don't deserve."

"Eat first." I interrupt, staring down at his joined hands with Kit. "You'll probably need both of those for that."

Kit frowns at her left hand, then jerks it back and folds her hands in her lap like she wasn't even aware she was touching him.

Bannik looks down at his left hand and squeezes it shut before opening it again. Pressed against his palm is a small piece of orange fur; it glows against his fingertips and then disappears altogether into his skin.

Alex clears his throat. "I didn't have the devil himself

sitting at dinner with a fox on one side and a Dark One on the other on my apocalypse bingo card; just saying."

"That's because you're stupid," Mason says helpfully.

Timber laughs. "We really try to have a positive morale around here."

"Cassius made us do a family-wide training once." Alex snorts. "Worst hour of my life, and I used to kill fairies." He flinches and turns to his wife. "Too soon, sorry, I'll just go get the spoon; you can spank me later."

"I think I just threw up," Ethan growls. "Keep your activities away from the dining room table."

"Should throw her on the dining room table and feast—"

Hope groans into her hands while Genesis makes a face and starts drinking her wine.

"Eat," Cassius says like it's the last meal any of us might have. "And then, fallen one, we will talk."

"Try not to fall asleep. It pisses him off," Alex says helpfully.

TWENTY-TWO

歳月人を待たず
Saigetsu hito o matazu
"Time and tide wait for no man."
Time flows without regard for humans' convenience.
-Japanese proverb

Kit

I've been sitting around the dinner table, trying to be normal. Trying to shove the past memories away while Horus just sits next to me as if my entire world hasn't just been revealed to me in the span of hours.

I taste him on my lips.

And then I *really* taste him.

I see him.

I feel him everywhere.

I also used to follow him everywhere. He would tell me stories of the stars, and I would tell him stories of the night. Why the night, of all things? The parts I feel like I'm supposed to remember get fuzzy whenever I think of the darkness, of being afraid of the moon and sleep.

Speaking of sleep, does that mean I'll actually be able to without having the same nightmares over and over again? Or will I succumb to the darkness?

What happens next? How does this end when all I keep seeing are images of us laced together with the bitterness of betrayal and loneliness?

Cassius takes a sip of tea. *I guess that's up to you, Kitsune.* He doesn't say it out loud, just stares into his tea like I'm the only one who can hear his thoughts.

My head aches, temples throb, so I try to focus on my inhales and exhales.

"Silly fox," Horus whispers from across the glade. "To think you can control the very air you breathe when all I have to do is exhale into the sky for you to fall."

"Exhale. Do it." I laugh. "And then hunt me. You'd like that, wouldn't you?"

"Hunting you or capturing you?" This arrogant god teases.

I shake my tails and run through the forests. I want this god to catch me. I know that he's not meant for me; we're from two very different worlds. He belongs in the past and has no place in my future.

The interesting thing about a certain destiny—you still fight it.

I know the ending before the beginning. He will never be mine, but maybe for just a short few weeks while he's stuck here, we can be something.

"How long?" I call back in a teasing tone. "How long are you stuck in my realm, god of the skies?"

His strides are long as he follows me through the trees. "A god is never truly stuck; it's more or less I got lost on the way to my destination."

"Poor baby."

"No." He releases a long sigh. "I'm feeling quite lucky, actually."

I stumble over a root and go headfirst into the water. I hate the water. It hurts my sensitive ears and makes me panic.

Strong arms grab me from behind and pull me out of the water and against the riverbank. "That desperate to escape me?"

I wiggle in his arms; the urge to shake my fur despite being back in human form is strong. I realize too late that since I'm back in my human form, I'm completely naked and wet against him.

A god shouldn't be touching me this intimately.

I shouldn't be liking it as much as I am, either. His fingertips dance along my arm, then touch my shoulder and swirl in circles. "The fur's pretty, but the skin is pretty too. You're soft everywhere, aren't you, fox?"

I sigh against him. Just a few more minutes, and then I'll pull away, just a few more moments of touching, and I'll pretend I hated it.

Instead, I turn in his arms, press my body against him, and close my eyes. It's hours later when I wake up. I'm covered in his black robe, still naked, lying on the forest floor, watching the flames of a fire lick higher and higher into the sky.

"Hungry?" he asks.

I sit up, and his robe instantly falls, revealing half my naked body. I quickly cover up again. "Sorry."

"Full moon." He points up at the sky with one of the sticks he is using to stoke the fire. "You'll be unable to transform back into fox form until it's gone, so I figured you needed at least a few clothes."

"Yeah." I gulp. "I normally stay in my cave, but it's loud there."

"Let me guess, you hate loud noises. Most foxes I've met do. Just like your ears are so sensitive, there's only one spot a male can touch that brings you pleasure."

My ears burn. "You know a lot about foxes, god out of time."

"I'm not out of time; I just took a detour, right? Besides, it's getting more and more interesting the more you talk."

I scowl. "I don't have time for this. I need to hunt."

"I'll hunt for you." He says it like It's simple and stands, dusting off his black leather pants. He's shirtless, with tattoos covering his left arm and another one specifically drawn across his left eye.

The Eye of Horus.

It's magical.

I look away. "You'll probably abandon me now."

"Never." His strong laugh seems to rustle the leaves on the trees overhead. "But if you're worried, you can always give me your bead for protection."

I gasp. "A fox never gives their most treasured possession! Least of all to a god who doesn't need it."

"It was a nice try." He laughs; it's a gentle sound that washes over me, caressing every inch of my body as sure as if he touched me with his hands. "Is it true that if you lose your fox bead forever, you'll have to prove your worth through three lifetimes as a human in order to gain the treasure back?"

I mentally curse and stare into the flames. "You're the god; you figure it out."

"So it's everything to you." He nods, and his eyes take on a faraway expression. "Good to know."

I sigh and decide to reveal, "My bead treats me the way your all-seeing eye treats you. Each of us is given something to *treasure, something that identifies us in this world and the next. To give up my bead would mean a lifetime of searching."*

"I wonder…" Horus whispers. "What could be so valuable that a fox would ever even consider it?"

I lick my dry lips. He's beautiful in the shadows of the fire and moon. His jaw firm, his white hair tucked down his back. He truly looks like a god.

"Yeah," I finally say. "I wonder what could possibly be worth it."

I don't tell him I'm looking at it, that I'd trade my bead for a kiss and steal it back in the same breath.

"Don't look at me like that," Horus says, his eyes burning into mine. "Not unless you plan on doing something about it."

I throw a stick and clear my throat. "It's forbidden, a deity with a lesser fox in the human realm. Why don't you just go back to where you belong, god? Don't you have an empire to run? The heavens? Go back to your own."

"Never truly liked my own." He grins smugly. "Let me go catch you some food. Fish okay?"

I love fish.

My stomach growls.

"Thought so…" He tilts his head. "A few berries sound good too?"

My damn stomach just doesn't quit.

Horus laughs. "You're very entertaining for a fox."

"You're very annoying for a god." I kick a rock that's in front of me, and his robe falls off my breasts again, causing him to laugh.

I grip it and clench my teeth. "Good luck fishing."

"Good luck sulking." He winks and starts walking away.

Insufferable creature.

I stick out my tongue and lean back against the forest floor, tugging his robe closer to my chilled body. It smells like the sky.

My eyes become heavy as sleep overtakes me.

Only to jerk me back to the present, staring around at the dining room table after seeing some of my memories and feeling the need to burst into tears.

I grip the edge of the table with my fingertips and start to slowly tap my thumb against the wood.

He visited for years.

He swore he'd die for me.

Then he left.

He never came back.

The number of lifetimes of suffering, of abandonment, only to be brought to this one moment at this table, staring at the god who failed me and wondering all along what I did wrong to love someone so deeply, to listen to as he spoke promises from his tongue—then never speak to me again.

I don't know why I lash out so hard other than the trauma pouring through my brain.

I kick Horus's chair.

Wine spits out of his mouth.

"And you? What do you have to say for yourself? Oh god of the sky that never came back."

Timber lets out a low whistle. "That... could be my fault. We did go back in time with Kyra to save her and the world, so that counts."

"It one hundred percent counts." Alex nods.

"It's weird when you agree with me," Timber grumbles under his breath.

Ethan sighs. "It won't last long, and you have Mason and Alex to thank for saving your sorry ass back in Egypt."

I kick his chair again. "You never came back!"

"Didn't she already say that?" Cassius asks not so quietly, then points at the basket in the middle of the table. "Are there any rolls left?"

I jump to my feet. "What is wrong with you people? I just got my memories back from being a freaking fox in a forest in Japan, and you guys are asking about dinner rolls?"

"Japan has forests?" Alex raises a hand. "Because I have questions."

Mason groans into his hands. "Why the hell would Japan have no forests?"

"Doesn't every country have forests?" Tarek pipes up.

"Holy shit!" Alex jumps back and falls out of his chair. "You've been here the whole time?"

Tarek flinches. "That was hurtful, and you know it."

"Sorry, bro." Alex lowers his head. "You were just so quiet."

"I had to chew." Tarek tugs at the last dinner roll and looks like he's purposefully eating slowly just to piss Cassius off. "Sorry, got the last one."

I kick back my chair and leave the room. They're all insane! How is every immortal impossible to live with?

Tears fill my eyes. I can almost feel my pretty tails then crumple to the ground in a heap at the top of the stairs when I remember that day.

She took them.

She wanted my bead, but I offered her something else.

I reach to my lower back, my fingers slowly grazing over the nine ridges.

I gave her my tails.

I gave my tails to see him again, even if it meant living three lifetimes; I gave over my nine tails, three for each lifetime.

I have no more tails left.

A fox without its tails can only transform if they have their bead and the bead only truly works with transformation when you have at least one tail left.

She asked for them all, which means I trapped myself and cursed myself at the same time, all in a vain effort to wait for a god who never returned.

Does he realize what I sacrificed to see him again? The hellish lifetimes I've lived through all in hopes that one day I'd be on equal footing with the god I'd fallen for?

"I waited in the forest for seven days," I whisper. "You promised you'd come back, but you never did. I didn't eat or sleep. The moon was a constant reminder of who you were, god of the sky who promised everything only to become a liar."

"I got trapped," Horus murmurs behind me. "You know that."

I ignore him and walk toward the first bedroom that doesn't look occupied and shut the door, closing him off just like I wish I could close off the pounding memories in my head of a man I loved too much.

And being the woman he loved too little.

TWENTY-THREE

弱肉強食
jakuniku kyoushoku
"The weak are meat" or "survival of the fittest"
~Japanese proverb

Horus

I chase after her. I was trying to give her time to process the memories flooding her, and because of my limited power, all I could do was watch the emotions cross her face. Our moments were private. They were part of a past I wish to forget yet also long to remember. Does she think this is easy on me just because I'm a god? That I don't care about our time together? Our friendship?

She thinks I left her. As if I would ever just leave her.

She doesn't realize I chose my brother and that the lives she lived without me didn't truly happen to me in the present. She suffered for centuries, and I simply skipped ahead in a moment.

She waited for me.

And all that time, I forgot about her until the memories

started flooding back, and now that my all-seeing eye is gone, all I have are the last few fragments of godhood in my body and the love I have for a little fox who used to play with me in the forest only to turn into a beautiful woman in the moonlight and tell me stories.

I was only supposed to stay in her forest for a week.

I stayed seven.

And promised to return on the eighth after Timber's joining.

And now, thousands of years later, I have a very pretty woman upset with me over promises I made in my past that I never carried through within our future.

I take the steps two at a time and find her at the top of them, touching her lower back and feeling her scars. I know what she feels there.

It would be like an angel getting its wings cut.

It would be like what happened to Bannik over and over again, a wound that will never heal and a reminder that will never stop, a reminder of your power of what you once were and a reminder you will never be that again.

She stands up and moves quickly, entering the bedroom. The door closes with an explosive *bang*.

I have to admit, I'm not used to getting doors slammed in my face. I raise my hand and knock. "Kit?"

"Why?" Her voice is muffled, but I can see the shadow of her feet in the bedroom light peeking underneath the door. "Why did you never come back? Was it really because of Timber?"

I sigh. "Kit, time shifted. One minute I was back in Egypt; the next, I was given a choice. Save my brother the way he's always saved me, allow him to survive and love, something he deserved after all his sacrifices in the underworld… or return to you. I won't lie. I would do anything for you, Kit. But when it came to my love for you and my love for my brother. I chose my brother."

"You forgot me."

"Time works differently when you're thrust out of it, Kit. I have memories flickers of our memories together. I went forward while you stayed back."

She jerks open the door. "Aren't I allowed to be angry that I was second choice to your brother? Aren't I allowed to be selfish for once in my life that I gave up everything for you? That I cut off my beautiful tails for a chance to see you again? She cut me!" Kit shrieks. "She would have killed me had I not traded with her!"

A tear slides down her cheek. It looks like a luminescent pearl. I reach for it, brushing it away softly. "You were very brave for a dumb fox."

"That's not funny." She shoves her hands against my chest. I grab her by the wrists and walk into the room, kicking the door shut behind me. "Let me go."

I release her hands, backing her up against the bed. "Do you think I've forgotten every heated summer night with you? How the water from the river would glisten off your naked body, tempting me day in and day out?"

She gulps and looks down, her eyes uncertain. "It was forbidden."

"I still looked," I admit softly. "I still touched you that one time. I still dreamed about it. Most people look to the stars and make a wish—I simply looked at you."

"Don't say things like that."

"Your kisses were always sweet."

"Sweet. Innocent." Kit's cheeks burn bright pink. "You were thousands of years older than me."

"Gross crush, Kit, even for a dumb fox."

"Stop calling me dumb fox!" She shoves my chest.

I grip her wrists again and spin her down onto the bed; her short dirty blonde hair hits the mattress, it's pink pieces glisten against the white duvet. "I would have gone through with it, I think. My self-control was already gone the day I left."

She squirms. I know it's embarrassing.

I wish I had my all-seeing eye so I could show it to her— the memory—to show her how adorable she looked when she asked me to be her mate in that forest.

The day before I left.

"I like this one the best." I run my palm along her orange and white tail. "It has character."

She flicks my hand away. "That's because I got it caught between two rocks while I was swimming."

"And nobody came to rescue you?" I pull her onto my chest. "Did you cry out to your family?"

She squirms beneath my touch. "What family? My entire den was—" Her breath hitches. "—anyway, I'm alone here, I have been for a while."

"Who taught you? Who cleaned your fur? Who helped you learn to shapeshift? Who caught your fish or collected your berries?"

She laughs. "I'm not an idiot; I did all that myself."

How tragic.

It's on the tip of my tongue to promise her that she'll never be alone again, but I can't see any of her destiny when I'm in her forest. All I see is darkness shrouding the stars above us, it is its own enchantment, and I'm careful to stay away from the very watchful eyes of the fallen angels guarding each territory. A god randomly walking around with a lesser deity is frowned upon.

Gods would hunt foxes in order to gain the power of their beads, and they'd try all sorts of tricks in order to gain more and more. And anyone watching could easily misunderstand and think all I want from this pretty little fox is what makes her special, when to me, what makes her special… is her.

The Creator eventually made seduction and luring of foxes forbidden.

But what the Creator clearly never took into consideration was foxes seducing the very gods that hunted them, and I'm very much seduced by this one.

"Horus." She presses me down onto the forest floor, soft with a cushion of pine needles, and crawls on top of me, straddling me on both sides. "Will you make me yours?"

It's asked so innocently I can't help but smile. "You're already mine."

"I mean…" She eyes me up and down. "…the real way, so I'm yours forever."

"Is this not real enough for you?" I ask. "Besides, you did just get your final tail; you have many things to explore."

"Stop always doing the right thing," she whines. "Just make me yours the way I know you want to."

I feel my eyes burn bright. "How can you tell?"

"I see the stars…" She presses a kiss to my forehead. "They're reflected in your eyes unless that's just a rumor."

I kiss her back. "You're young, Kitsune."

"Then wait for me."

I nod. "I'll wait for you, and I'll come back for you."

She rests her head on my chest. "Then you'll make me yours in every way?"

"Yes." I vow it to her, but I refrain from saying a promise I'm not sure I can or should keep.

A god should never fall for a fox.

The temptation is too great.

But I fell that day in the forest.

Never once thinking about the power others sought, and only of the girl that held it in her soul.

Kit shoves me, bringing me back to the present. "Stop thinking."

"What am I thinking of?"

"That day." She clenches her teeth. "You were right. I was young and stupid to even think you would wait for me; the great and mighty Horus returned to his sky and left his little fox to die, sounds like a children's rhyme."

"I would definitely not read that to my children."

"Get away." Tears fill her eyes. "Please."

"I think…" I lower my head. "I'll stay."

"Don't mean it." Her lower lip trembles.

"I wasn't there then, but I'm here now, and I'm not returning to the sky or choosing anyone but you."

"All gods lie."

"Gods are incapable of lying unless their souls are black." I point out. "So no, I'm not lying."

She squeezes her eyes shut. "What? Now you're just going to make me yours, and we'll forget all the memories of the forest and the—"

I swallow her next words.

Her small gasp is more like a meow, which makes it

impossible for me not to smile against her mouth. "Once a fox, always a fox."

I drag my hands down her sides brushing against her soft skin, lifting her shirt higher and higher until her hand touches mine, stopping me. "Are you, a god, breaking the rules and seducing a fox?"

"I don't see a fox; I see a beautiful woman. Besides, it's not like I have a lot of goodness left in me."

"I'm still insulted," she whispers, her eyes greedily staring at my mouth.

I rub my thumb across her lower lip. "Is that why you're purring?"

"I do not—"

"You do." I correct her and press my hand to her chest. "I can feel it."

She knows I'm right, she knows I can feel her body's response as well as hear it, and I love that she has no way of denying it.

I duck my head against her neck and run my nose up and down her sensitive skin, then kiss the outside of her ear. The purring intensifies, a rumble in her chest she can't stop.

The louder she gets, the more control of whatever fragments I still barely cling to disappear.

I grab her by the waist and pull her fully onto the bed. Her small hands cup my face as I keep kissing down her neck. I had forgotten how good her skin tastes, like the very rich forest she used to live in, fresh like rain in the morning, the woods outside, and then sweet like a warm summer night.

My tongue slides across her collarbone. Her body jumps beneath me, and her hands move to my shoulders like she needs to anchor herself against me.

I rise up above her. "Did you mean it?"

"Wh-what?"

"That you want to be mine?"

Her eyes dart back and forth in uncertainty before she slowly nods her head. "I'm still angry. But I never stopped wanting you—"

I silence her with a kiss. "Good, be angry as much as you want, we have lifetimes left for your anger, but tonight can you just be mine?"

Her hands reach for my black shirt, and she tugs it over my head. Our foreheads almost collide when I grab her T-shirt and do the same.

I may be limited, but I can at least do one thing for her right now, and it's not give her myself—it's to give her what she wants, the moment she wants it.

I wave my right hand across her face, knowing it might be the last godlike thing I do in this lifetime, giving her back her home.

Her eyes widen. "My forest!"

"Our forest." I smile.

"How did you—"

"It's just a memory., I say with a sad shake of my head. "But I figured you would be most comfortable if you felt like you were at your home."

A tear runs down her face. "I haven't been back here since—"

"I know." I smile and tuck her hair over her shoulder. "I may not be as powerful without my eye, but I can, at the very least, give you a vision of your home while I show you why you've always been mine."

"Modern times have changed you." She actually laughs.

"You know how to seduce way better."

"Was I horrible before?"

"You yelled at me." She points out. "And told me that a dumb fox shouldn't be so close to the town border, then yelled the next day that I was too close to the water as if I can't swim."

"I saved you from drowning."

"Swimming," she corrects and flips me onto my back.

The feeling is so familiar, being in her forest, flirting with her, wanting to take her, kiss her, then take her again.

Nothing is stopping me now.

Maybe losing my eye was all worth it—for this trade.

For my own little Kitsune.

"I'm trapped now." I smile up at her. "What will you do with me?"

"Ah, I trapped my own god, lucky me." She points a finger at me. "Still angry."

"Still allowed," I answer.

She rests her chin on my chest. "I missed the smell of the sky."

"I missed the darkness of your forest."

Her eyes brighten, flashing orange. She's beautiful. She seems free now, her smile wide and innocent.

I lean in to kiss her again, but she pulls back and jumps to her feet. Her eyes are teasing, sly. She shoves her shorts to the ground kicking them away before peeling off the rest of her clothes and facing me.

She's perfect.

Her stomach is silky and curved, her hips are made for my hands, and every inch of her reminds me of how soft her skin has always been.

"Come here," I command.

"I will." Her eyes are nervous before she puts her hands over her head and does a small twirl. "But first, you get your dance."

My jaw hangs open. I don't want to tell her she can't do a fox mating dance without tails, but apparently, it doesn't matter because the minute she starts moving her hips back and forth, my mouth goes dry.

Her eyes close, and she runs her hands down her body while I slowly make my way over to where she's dancing.

I grip her by one of her wrists and spin her face forward against the closest tree and pin her there. "Mine."

She arches her back against me, I protect her with my body. The feel of the sky watching this only pushes me past the edge of control. She lets out a soft cry when I flip her back around and meet her mouth with a possessive kiss. I can almost imagine her tails, soft against my legs, my cheek, only to disappear and reveal herself to me as if saying take me, I'm yours, I'm terrified, but let me reveal myself to you, without the guise of magic, without anything but myself.

Bare.

Just like she is now.

Foxes never allow their tails, their shields of magic, to leave their bodies until they let someone in. And even though she no longer has tails to move. I feel it mentally, spiritually. She's open to me.

Mine.

Her tongue is hot and wet, aggressively massaging mine in a way that feels like an urgent caress I can't wait to answer. I grab one of her legs and wrap it around me like she's a dancer and I'm her pole. I groan as the heat between her open legs rubs a moist path along my hip until she is snugged against my waist. My cock twitches, desperately wanting more, needing it in a way that feels so holy I have a hard time breathing. I realize I'm afraid… this moment terrifies me. I don't want to scare her, but I wonder if I maybe need her more than she needs me. I've needed this for thousands of years, looked forward to it, and she seems so open I don't want to let her down. I'm afraid. I'm so afraid that I'm going to be too much for her, that something bad might happen afterward. What if sleeping with a god is her demise? She doesn't even have her tails anymore.

I sigh against her mouth.

She shoves my chest. "Take me, stupid god."

"Okay, dumb fox." I laugh. I have no other choice but to give in to this beautiful woman, this human, fox without her tails, this person who I've known across lifetimes, one I abandoned without realizing the ramifications.

Her smile's sad as she reaches for me, her fingers twist into my hair, wrapping it around her fingertips. "You're so easy to love."

"I'm not."

She twists harder and pulls my face into hers. Our lips collide. "You are. You're easy to love because you are good."

"Because I'm light?"

"Because you protected a stupid fox after she saved you and because when she was the most lonely in the world— you asked her what she saw."

Tears burn the back of my eyes. "And what did you see?"

"Stars. So many stars. You pointed to the sky and said that my parents were shining, and then my own darkness just felt less. I felt less, in the best way, because you were my light."

"I never deserved to be that." I choke out. "I wanted you. I was selfish."

"Then take me, selfish god of the sky." She releases my hair suddenly and spreads her arms wide, laying on her back. "Take me the way I wanted you to, under the stars. Let them hear me scream for you."

I love her bravery. I lean over and whisper, "Are you sure you want that, little fox?"

"Are you sure you can take me?"

We're both panting. She's pressed so hard against me I can feel every heated part of her waiting for me to make a choice I can't unmake. Seduce the fox and live. Walk away and be miserable.

"You were made for this." I take her mouth, capturing her lips in a punishing kiss, her hands are suddenly back at my hair, pulling it like it's hers, not mine, and I realize she has a fixation with it.

Because to her, my hair is fur.

And with foxes, you groom their fur when you mate. So as she twists her hands into my hair, tugging it and wrapping it around her fingers, meeting my lips with each painful tug. I realize it was always supposed to be like this. With each punishing kiss from her mouth, each slick of her tongue down my neck. It was supposed to be painful. Joining with her, knowing she owns me as much as I own her. Knowing our pasts. Aligning our futures.

We will not be able to undo this.

I would never want to.

I almost collapse against her when she shoves her legs against the tree and pulls me back, flipping me midair onto the ground.

I laugh. "Playful."

"For being such an old god, you have good reflexes."

I shove her against the ground, rising up over her. My body flexes and stretches over her. I could enter her. I could end this so easily; I could make her mine, instead, I just watch.

Is that not the purpose of stars? Gods? Angels?

I smile down at her. "How pretty."

"What?"

"Your face," I whisper seconds later. "Before," I inch forward between her thighs. "I make you mine before I truly watch."

"Me?"

"Oh yes." I press my body down onto hers and thrust between her thighs. Kit's eyes widen, her hands fall back from my hair, then grip my shoulders. "And now I truly watch Heaven. The crown of creation." My lips meet hers. "My mate."

She gasps beneath me, her eyes roll back into her head only to come back full of bright white stars that erupt around us.

I see constellations.

Her.

Us.

She grasps me close. My hips take on a different rhythm, the rhythm of the heavens, as I slowly show her what I feel, what I felt then, what I feel now.

Her little gasps against my mouth make it worth it. "I see everything."

"I see you."

"The stars." She nibbles my lower lips and moans. "It

feels so good, having all of you, and yet knowing the sky watches."

"It sees everything."

"And yet, all I see is you," she responds as he rakes her nails down my arms and pulls me closer.

I'm deep into the cosmos, into her, my body taking over, and my soul is finally silent.

It's home.

She pulls me close, tight, almost too tight; deeper and deeper, we fall and explore until I don't know how to stop the collision of our bodies.

And like a supernova.

We explode together.

And I swear in that moment, with her body pulsing beneath me and all around me, I see the stars I used to create, I feel them.

I just wish I knew if it was a good omen.

Or if we just damned ourselves again.

TWENTY-FOUR

人生において 最も大切な時 それはいつ でも いまです

Jinsei ni oite mottomo taisetsu na toki sore wa itsu demo ima desu

The most important time in life is always the present.

~ Mitsuo Aida, Japanese poet and calligrapher

Kit

I didn't expect this. I had no clue it would feel this good, that *he* would feel this good, or that it would be this right.

My tongue tastes of the sky, and I have no way to describe it other than it's something so sweet, like tasting chocolate before it goes bitter, then feeling it sink into you, motionless as you rest in its flavor.

He's Horus… I shouldn't be surprised. But he's also a god, and I realize I've mostly forgotten this as I lay naked against his chest.

Horus licks up my neck as if he knows that foxes love to be licked and comforted, and then he pulls me tighter against him. "You'll see; it's all going to be okay."

I'm with him.

I'm now half of him. Of course, it's going to be okay. How could it not be? I cuddle next to him and finally allow myself to let go and sleep.

I don't know if it's hours later or minutes, but I wake up to voices. I think it's Horus and maybe Timber? I have no clue, but I go downstairs to grab some water and smile to myself at the fact that all the immortals argue as if they've been living together since the dawn of time.

They're truly a family.

And I love them even more for it.

Because I finally have a family of my own in them.

I feel it inside my chest, ready to burst free. I have a place to belong. Maybe the forest wasn't my home after all, maybe it too was a test, and now I get to be free with a werewolf I would have tried to kill or run from, a vampire who breathes terror, fallen ones, sirens, gods.

I smile even harder. I knew this world existed, but it was never a part of mine, and now that it finally is, I find I'm not afraid of the moon anymore. I'm not afraid of anything except for losing the one I've been waiting for.

Him.

I tiptoe over to the sink and reach up to grab a glass. My hand hesitates when I hear Timber.

"You know…"

I believe it's Horus who sighs. "No, I don't know, what?"

"You could take it."

"Take what?"

"Her bead," Timber says simply. "Your power would be restored completely in this timeline. You'd be close to as powerful as Cassius, could probably save a lot of people, help the balance between the immortals and the humans."

Horus is quiet. Why isn't he saying anything? Finally, he speaks after what feels like an eternity. "I'm here to help her know who she is, not to take the one last thing that gives her immortality and her power. She's without her tails. She can't be without both. It would turn her into a human, and we have no idea how long she would have."

"She could give it willingly." Timber suggests. "Save the masses, kill the few."

"What's wrong with you?" Horus shouts. "I actually care for her!"

"It's one tiny fox, Horus."

"Don't make me regret saving you."

Timber laughs. "Sometimes it's too easy, brother, relax. All I'm saying is—" I don't hear the rest of what he does say. I'm too pissed off. I trusted Timber, but of course, that was a stupid move. I really am a stupid fox. How can you trust the god of the underworld in the first place?

Livid, I stomp up the stairs and slam the door to the room I was just in, sitting on the mattress stewing, ready to punch a god in the face.

Of course, my fox bead would give him power. Isn't that why it's forbidden for a god to seduce a fox now? It would give them too much access to what I have, the purity of the earth and the sky.

I'm a fox of darkness, after all, of night. If I gave the god of the skies my bead, he'd have both.

I gasp awake.

"Wha…?"

Had I been having a nightmare that entire time?

Horus is leaning over me, concern etched in his bright

blue eyes. I could almost imagine he looks like my very own star, watching over me, keeping me safe. "I thought you no longer had nightmares in the presence of a god?"

I touch my mouth with my fingertips. "Did we just kiss, or was I dreaming?"

His eyes are full of mischief; they flicker like Christmas lights. "Yes. I leaned down and kissed you gently… I hope you don't mind I—"

"It's a full moon." I interrupt, probably rudely. "Right? It's still a full moon?"

"I think so." He frowns and looks out the window. "It appears we're on our last night of it. You have no reason to be afraid anymore." His frown deepens. "You look really pale. Do you need water or—" His eyes roll to the back of his head, but he regains focus and presses his palms against his temples. "Sorry, I think I'm just tired."

"Gods get tired?" I ask, trying to lighten the mood.

"Apparently, now they do." He leans down next to me and pulls me against his chest. Why does it feel like things are about to get more difficult? "At least I'm here."

I'm afraid to ask, but I do anyway. "And if I close my eyes when I open them… you'll still be here. You won't leave me?"

Horus scoffs and waves me away with a hand that suddenly falls against the down comforter like he's so exhausted he can barely keep it up. "Where else would I go?"

"The sky." I point up to the ceiling. My breath feels heavy, and my body the same. Something is happening, but I don't know what it is. I just breathe in and out and stare up as if I can see the stars through the ceiling. "Am I yours, Horus?" I ask, my voice somehow sounding small to my ears.

"Yes."

"Is what's mine also yours?"

He frowns and leans down on the bed, making it sag toward him. I roll into his massive chest and reach for his neck, my fingers grasping his white-blond hair. He's so beautiful, still glowing a bit from our time together. "What's mine is yours, what's yours is mine. You asked me long ago to make it happen, and we did. I want to spend forever with you."

"And you would never betray me?"

His frown is so sincere I feel bad asking. He jerks back, but I hold him close, making him stay against me.

"Why would you ask that?"

"I heard you," I whisper. "Downstairs."

He shakes his head. "My brother's going to get his ass beat. I have no idea what he was talking about, but either way, I'm guessing you didn't hear everything he said since you left angry."

So he knew I was there.

"All he said," Horus continues, "was that I need to tell you one thing." His eyes flash white.

Tears burn the back of my throat. "What's that?"

His eyes falter, going from white to black and then back again. He covers his left eye where the tattoo is but no eye remains, and clenches his teeth. "No, no, no, no!"

"Horus?"

"Help." His body trembles. "Cover my mouth. COVER IT!"

I clap both hands over it, but he shoves me away easily, collapsing backward onto the floor. Thunder booms in the distance like a bad omen from the heavens themselves. He suddenly stands and walks over to me. His eyes don't reflect the sky anymore—they reflect my darkness. *"Give it to me, give me what I'm owed, fox of the night."*

"Never." I kick at his chest.

He grips me by the ankle and jerks me down the bed. I can tell he has no clue what's going on. His one eye is black. Someone else is seeing through it, using his power to see through the remaining eye.

I need to fight him at all costs.

He's not himself.

And yet he rips every piece of clothing from me and shoves me against the bed. "Mine, my star, you're mine, fight it, fight us!"

I can't though. I can't fight what we are to each other as his kisses become power-hungry against my neck, only to have him inch by inch bite down my skin.

"Horus," I whimper. "It's good, but it's wrong, what are you doing?"

He jerks away, his head shakes, and then he's jumping away from me, slamming back against the wall like I've stunned him stupid.

Was that even Timber downstairs?

"HELP!" I scream. "Someone help us!"

Horus gets to his feet. His chuckle is dark and sinister; it's not what I'm used to... all the warmth in him has been sucked away from the room. "You should be more careful what you give to people, and so should he..."

His mouth bruises mine, again and again, holding me captive, pinning me against the bed with fervor like he loves me, but this isn't him—this is a god possessed. "Give me what I'm owed, fox of darkness, and part those pretty little lips."

A choking sensation washes over me. I can't speak. I can only cough over and over again. It burns from my toes all the way up to my neck. Grasping for Horus, I wait for him to save me. For my old Horus to come back to fight whatever monster that's using him.

But he doesn't.

His one eye is blank with nothingness.

The other is missing. Even his tattoos pulse on his left cheek like he's trying to break free, but what can a limited god do against someone using my bead along with my tails, using any sort of power against him?

"Apophis," I whisper.

Another laugh escapes his lips. "Smart girl, now open up."

I kick him in the legs, but I'm not strong enough. His body crashes onto mine, his lips take hold, biting down into me, leaving tiny marks of blood. I taste its tang as it runs down my throat when he says. "Open."

I can't keep it down.

My bead floats softly to my tongue and rests there. In any other circumstance, I would love his kiss right now, the way his tongue massages mine, but I know it's only to bring the bead closer, so he keeps massaging, keeps sucking on the blood from my lips.

The only way to bring a bead out is through a kiss, but blood always has to be spilled. Mine.

He sucks my lips dry until they feel swollen. Green and yellow light erupts from my mouth.

My bead. What makes me immortal, powerful, special—has just been torn from my body by the very man I love.

He has betrayed me twice.

Once on purpose.

The second by idiocy, because in giving his eye, there will always be someone who can see through the other.

Idiots.

All of us.

I fall back against the mattress and start to shake. My body is no longer immortal. My power is gone. I'm nothing but a human shell with scars that used to show my glory.

And the person who took it all from me was the one I waited for and trusted the most in the world.

I burst into tears. The pain is nearly unbearable as the bead of energy leaves my body and enters his. Horus's chuckle is dark and lonely; he falls to his knees and collapses into a heap against the floor.

I jump after him. Maybe if I pry his mouth open.

A hand jerks out and shoves me away. The energy from his palm is green; he moves to his knees and stares me down. "What the hell have you done?"

"I have no idea!" I yell. "Do you even know what *you* just did? You kissed me, you stole my bead—"

He shoves me away from him. "Stay back!" He holds his hands out in front of him, tiny flecks of green and yellow fire burn from his palms. His skin looks like the sun mixed with the earth; it turns dark every few seconds like the night sky. He trembles on the floor, his one eye flickers black and blue. "We need to get it out of me!" Voice hoarse, he collapses against the floor again. "Get Cassius, now! Get Timber, get everyone!"

"It won't kill you!" I yell. "It's going to kill me!"

"Exactly!" He laughs again, then catches himself and shakes his head. "I'll kill you without thinking twice; I can't be both darkness and light." He curses. "She made me a monster. She used my eye to make me a tool. Her own god of monsters."

Well done, I want to say. He goes to sacrifice to give me my past back and, with his sacrifice, steals our future.

I refuse it.

I rebuke it.

"No!" I yell. I have no power left, though, but I do have legs. I sprint past him, open the door and collide with Bannik.

"And the prince of the sky will become more than a god, pissing off the heavens and hell all at once, I think, is how the nursery rhyme goes." Bannik leans against the doorjamb. "I knew you wanted something from her."

"No." Horus shakes his head. "I didn't want her power. That's not what happened. She could see through my eye. She tricked me, waited until I was weak until I gave myself to Kit."

"It doesn't matter, you idiot. Did I not warn you?" Bannik slams his hands against the wall by the door. A picture falls, and the glass shatters into rubble by his black boots. "Your very existence is about balance. How can darkness and light co-exist? It is a balance you have just disrupted. A fox can survive without her tails, but a fox without her bead will eventually die. So much for a happy ending."

Tears stream down my face. He's not wrong. I am the fox of the night, and losing my bead to the light means eventual death.

"I'll give it back," Horus says through clenched teeth. "I just need a minute to think." He rams his hands through the wall next to me. Everything turns to dust around us, coating the carpeting at our feet.

His godhead in this timeline has fully returned ten times what it once was. He's dangerous. Powerful. And he's angry.

It's up to me to calm him down, and Bannik isn't helping.

"Hey…" I reach for Horus only to have Bannik shove me behind him. "Just let me talk to him."

"He's going to either die getting the bead out of him or become a fallen, either way, you can't help him. All he can do is help himself." Bannik shakes his head. "Never listen to the voices, Horus. Even if they make sense."

"I just wanted to kiss her, then a sweet voice said to bite down."

"That sweet voice was Apophis, and she's come to collect her final sacrifice." He looks between both of us and shakes his head. "You. She wants you, Horus. She already has your eye, and now that you're powerful in this timeline, she wants you to do all her bidding. Even Cassius couldn't fight you now." He laughs. "Wow, and I thought I'd be the end of the Immortal Council. Meanwhile, the Egyptian god of gods has me hold his beer."

"I'm not laughing."

"Because it's not funny!" Bannik yells.

Ethan slams his hands against the door. "Why is everyone yelling?"

"Oh, shit," Alex says behind him. "He pulled a full god."

I try to take deep breaths but have nothing. Bannik pulls me against his side and hides me from Horus, using his body to guard me. "Leave."

"And go where?" Cassius says quietly at the door. "To the very demoness that wants him? There has to be a way to help him. Until then." He nods to Mason and Alex.

I frown. What can they do?

Timber walks in, late to the party. "What did I miss?"

"YOU!" I yell. "I heard what you said to Horus downstairs."

Timber holds up his hands. "I was at the twenty-four-hour mini-mart down the road getting ice cream, so I don't know what you think I did. Apologies if you wanted vanilla, most people around here like strawberry."

"Shit." Bannik releases a string of curses. "She used a phantom on you. She must have been collecting more beads. She always uses the same one, weird hair, tattoos down his arms, attractive and alluring. Ring a bell?"

Timber drops the groceries in his hand. An apple tumbles toward me, hitting my foot. I don't know why I fixate on it, but the apple represents something so simple, and now everything is complicated. Now that I've found joy, I have nothing but an unhappy ending.

"You should have never come back," I find myself saying. "Horus should have never looked for me, and I should have never sacrificed for him." Tears burn my eyes and threaten to fall. "We were never meant to be in the first place. A god will always seduce a fox even if he's all-powerful, and a fox will always give everything to their god." I jerk away from Bannik and walk down the stairs, one by one until I'm outside.

When I finally walk at least a half mile down the dirt road, I fall to my knees, then look up at the stars and scream.

TWENTY-FIVE

猪突猛進

English Translation:
"Charge headlong."

-Japanese proverb

Horus

I'm tied to a chair.

Bannik's pacing in front of me with Cassius behind him, still as a statue. The rest of the girls and the kids have been sent away.

I'm basically with nothing but angry immortals being stared at like I'm the plague, and nobody knows where Kit is.

"Let me at least try to find her," I say.

Bannik's answer is to kick my chair back. "You stole her bead!"

"Not on purpose!" I yell. "We just need to give it back!"

"Idiots," Cassius growls. "All of you." His normally pale skin pinks at his cheeks. "Did you take her?"

"Huh?" Alex asks. "Take her? Where the hell would he take her?"

"Take her where? McDonald's?" Mason asks.

Ethan curses, Bannik joins in, and Tarek walks into the room and mutters, "He means sex, dumb and dumber."

Timber follows in after him. "If he had sex with her, then she was vulnerable, maybe vulnerable enough that if he spoke an incantation, she was able to weasel her way through the eye he gave up to pull the bead."

I jolt to my feet, the chair still attached to me. "And you didn't think that was important information?"

The ropes burst free from my arms while the chair crashes into splinters onto the ground.

Timber holds out a hand and takes a sip of his coffee; Alex joins in, I'm suddenly held by two powerful gods in golden rope that burns every inch of my skin with every breath.

"Sit," Timber commands.

I don't.

He sighs and gives Alex a *"help out"* look. Alex rolls his eyes and snaps his fingers. A chair comes from behind while gravity forces me down.

Bannik takes a step backward against the wall.

"I think you're scaring the fallen angel." Mason yawns. "Okay, information. We need information. How can you get the bead back to her without going all dark and brooding on us?"

The room falls quiet. Not exactly promising.

"I never wanted it," I say. "I just wanted her. I wanted her for an eternity. I don't even remember taking it."

Bannik pulls out a chair next to me. "She gave up her nine tails, right?"

My stomach drops. "Right. Which means she's basically lost as a human right now and could easily die."

"Killjoy," Ethan mutters.

"Not what I was getting at, vampire!" Bannik slams his fists against the dinner table. It collapses onto the floor, all four of the legs shattered.

"And another one bites the dust," Alex sings, earning a groan from Cassius.

Tarek kicks at the dust on the ground and grabs the remaining chair, flipping it around and straddling it. "Why the nine tails, big guy?"

A thick silence descends over the living room before Bannik answers. "If she has her nine tails, hell if she had two tails, she could pull the bead back in, only if it's with someone who's… mated with her."

I gulp.

The room goes quiet again.

Alex raises his hand. "So I think the question is, did you two—"

"You didn't hear them?" Timber laughs. "Why else do you think I left for ice cream?"

"I put on headphones," Mason admits.

"I was watching Dateline," Cassius grumbles.

"And I was out for a run while Bannik stewed in the backyard," said Tarek. "He walked on your tomato plant, by the way, Timber."

"Son of a bitch, Bannik!"

"I SLIPPED!" he yells.

"SILENCE!" Cassius looks ready to throw something. "So the way to solve this is easy, we'll go with Horus to the Abyss, grab the tails and come back."

"No." Bannik's hoarse voice sends chills down my spine. "He can't just steal them back. He'll have to earn them. And even if he can fight and win, the Abyss doesn't let you go without the sacrifice. His, I'm sad to say, will be time."

"How much?" I ask.

"For her? For us? A few weeks."

I squeeze my eyes shut. "And for me?"

"Nine tails equal three lifetimes, Horus. You're looking at three hundred years at the very least."

I stand, mind made up. I grab a piece of paper and start to write. Minutes later, I'm folding it up and handing it to Bannik. "Make sure she looks up from time to time."

"You're not going to say goodbye?" Timber asks. "To her? To any of us?"

"Why say goodbye when I'll be back?"

"Terminator." Tarek nods. "Classic."

"How can you joke right now?" Timber lunges for him.

Tarek grins, his eyes flicker with blue. "Ah, we all have our reasons for doing what we do. Sometimes, we have to walk through the darkness in order to find our true light. Good luck, Horus. We'll keep watch." His eyes fall to Bannik. "It is, after all, what you do, isn't it?"

Bannik pales. "What?"

"Watcher." Cassius's voice booms. "You watch. You do not look away from your purpose, from your being. Will you *watch her?*"

A tear slides down Bannik's cheek. His whisper is haunting. "May I die if I close my eyes just once."

"You did, though," Cassius says quietly. "But now I wonder what will happen when the one who chose her, who watched her, is back?"

"What?" I ask.

Bannik shakes his head. "I watched the mountain."

"Yes." Cassius smiles sadly. "But before you watched the mountain, you watched a tiny innocent little fox fall into a river. You kept her safe when her parents died and when the last of those who loved her left—you made a pact with the heavens, and you finally chose."

Tears stream down Bannik's face. "What did I choose then if you're so smart?"

Cassius waves his hand in front of us, a star shines so brightly down on Kit, she's lying across the grass and reaches for the star, whispering, "I choose you too, pretty star. Keep me safe."

The star shoots across the sky and places itself above her.

"Don't you see?" Cassius sighs. "Things always come full circle. You, Bannik, before you fell, before you stopped watching, were her star. Why else would the Creator place you at her mountain? In Asia?"

Bannik falls to his knees and screams.

I squeeze my eyes shut. "It's why she reached for your hand."

Bannik doesn't speak; he just stares at his hands as if they're dirty like he doesn't deserve to know even the good he did.

I sigh. "You have your job back."

He nods his head and stands. "I won't let you down this time. I will not fall."

I believe him.

His shaky hand comes out to grip mine. I shake it hard. "Make sure she watches." I shove the note into his hand.

And I take my slow walk to the Euphrates to descend into The Abyss.

This time, I didn't choose my brother.

I didn't choose me.

I willingly choose her, even if it means years of torture. I'll stay, and I'll endure. What's three hundred years to her three lifetimes of not knowing what she was?

I smile as I walk.

And when I reach the muddy bed, I have enough power that I simply flick open the gated window and hold out my hands. "Kings of The Abyss—you have permission to imprison me."

Chains drag against the ground, they get caught on rocks and objects. They get closer and closer.

Cold metal clasps around my wrists. "You are out of your time, god."

"No." I shake my head. "I think I'm actually exactly where I'm supposed to be."

TWENTY-SIX

悪戦苦闘
akusenkutou
"An uphill battle."
–Japanese proverb

Kit

I fall to the dirt, my knees hit the ground hard enough to make them bruise; I know I'll be picking pieces of the dirt away from them later.

I'm betrayed again.

He's all-powerful, and I'm going to die. I guess every being dies, mortal or not, something always happens, but I'll die sooner than later after trusting him.

Trusting all of them.

I stare up at the sky, but all I see is darkness. Maybe I finally see what I feel, and now that I don't have a star that feels it with me, I have no guilt in saying I'm sad, alone, isolated, angry.

It's like a shroud of blackness that makes it impossible to see the stars. I reach up with trembling fingertips and then drop my hands to the ground.

I have no tails.

No bead.

I'm nothing anymore.

I want to believe it was an accident, but what about the conversation with Timber?

I crawl toward the closest tree I can find and huddle beneath it, hugging my knees to my chest. It's Seattle, so of course, it starts to rain, though I'm protected.

A dark figure appears down the road. I immediately recognize Bannik. Great, just what I need, a fallen angel giving me advice on how to live when he's been kept down in the Abyss for who knows how long?

He crouches down next to me. "Can I sit?"

"Can you? Sure. Do I want you to? No."

"Foxes, always so honest despite everyone saying how much they manipulate mankind."

"You're no man."

He barks out a laugh and throws his red and black hair over his shoulder. "What gave me away?"

His eyes still have pieces of white and red in them; they fade to black every time he shifts. "What used to be in your eyes?"

He stills. "What do you mean?"

"Horus is a god of the sky, you're a fallen, and your job was to watch, so what did your eyes reflect?"

His normal scowl turns into a small smile, transforming his face. He looks beautiful, almost ethereal. I can see him in his golden armor, proud, standing on the mountain the watchers or fallen guarded, all before deciding they wanted humanity as their own.

All before they fell.

For love.

"Well…" He leans back against the tree and crosses his arms over his chest. He looks so normal again, wearing a simple black trench coat, a white shirt, and jeans with black boots. "Our eyes reflect what we worship."

"What?"

"As angels, our eyes reflect what we worship. Imagine looking away from your only job, knowing you were to look straight to the heavens and watch, never blink, simply watch… the minute your eyes fall away from their purpose, something else is breathed into existence in your line of sight, and it gets harder and harder to look back to your purpose until you finally forget what it actually is in the first place." He looks to the stars. "Your eyes will reflect your worship, Kit. If his eyes reflected the stars, if they reflected you—he's good. If they reflected the bead, you would have seen it. It would have been impossible for him to hide it."

"So why did he—"

"The all-seeing Eye of Horus. You know the stories?"

She nodded. "Some."

"Apophis probably found a way to use his eye and see into yours, to put him in a trance and take one final treasure, one final sacrifice. Remember, the gods and goddesses used to hunt for you."

I nod, wringing my hands together. "You never hunted me."

"Because my job was to protect your forest. To protect everything in it, humans, foxes, cows—"

"I'm better than a cow or human," I grumble.

"Apologies." He holds up his hands. "I just thought it would be good to discuss moving forward."

I stop feeling sorry for myself for one instant. "What do you mean moving forward?"

He reaches for my hand and holds it tight. "It was me. I was your star."

"What?" I can barely get the word out. "My star? You?"

"It's why you wanted to touch me that first night. I was reborn, returned to you, the very little fox I watched and protected before I guarded the mountain before I fell. When I was sent to your mountain, I watched you more, but with each passing year, my star diminished more and more, not because of you but because of me. It made you feel more lonely; we felt each other's emotions. It should have been a warning for you, but you had no family—all you had was Horus to protect you, so when I finally did fall into the Abyss, you had hope that one day the god of the sky would return. Why else do you think you fell for him? Your star was gone. But, you were given the whole sky." He smiles at me sadly. "I would have wished that for you. I'm glad that was your future, Kit." He reaches into his pocket and hands me a small piece of paper. "And now, we might have to journey together without the sky, but I promise, your star will never again choose to fall unless it's for the greater good of the life you deserve."

I slowly unfold it, tears running down my cheeks.

Look to the skies. I'll always exist there for you. And when you can't feel me, speak to the wind: it whispers your name. My love for you will span lifetimes just like yours did for me. Wait for me, and if you can't—know that I'll always exist in the stars. And so will you. Take care of your star—make him shine the way you shine for me.

"What?" I crumple up the piece of paper. "What's this? A goodbye? Is he dying? What's happening?"

Bannik turns his head slowly, cranes it like he's truly examining me; his eyes burn blue, he doesn't even blink, and all I see in the reflection of his face is my own, like a mirror being held open to me. "We watch."

"What? Why are you watching me?"

He takes something from his pocket and jerks it across his palm, two drops of blood fall to the dirt. "I have no reason to ask this, Creator, but can you please show her just once… the stars beneath her darkness?"

The earth beneath me starts to rumble, and singing erupts around me like I'm in my own fairytale. The darkness above slowly falls to a mist around me into tiny fireflies. When I blink up, I see the stars.

"Look." Bannik points. "He never truly forgot about you, little fox." His laugh is soft, softer than I imagined it would be. "Do you think a god would leave a mere note under the pillow for you? He is a god, Kitsune. He doesn't do things by half measures, and by my estimation…" His smile is beautiful and wide, almost like this moment is as much for him as it is for me. "He created this the day he left to return home just in case something happened."

"What? What did he create?" I'm panicking, staring at the stars, wondering, waiting.

"Only the god of the skies can manage to puzzle together constellations…" He sighs in relief. "Watch."

His hand waves in front of us, pushing more of the dark mist back, and in the middle of the sky, I don't just see stars… I see a constellation of them.

In the shape of a fox.

"Look to the stars," Bannik says again. "And until he returns, I'll do what he asked me to do."

"He's gone?" I whisper. "To do what?"

"Find a way to gain your tails, return your bead, right what's been wrong… he's gone to the Abyss."

I jump to my feet, but Bannik pulls me back down. "Let me go!"

"It's his destiny."

"And yours?"

Bannik's quiet for a few seconds, then locks eyes with me. "He gave me my purpose back."

"To be annoying?"

He grabs my hand and squeezes it. "To watch."

"Who?" My throat's so thick it's hard to breathe.

"You know who." He nods. "Maybe I won't mess up this time."

"He could die."

"We all could. Immortality is a joke." He grunts and falls to his back, staring up at the sky. "Until then, you should watch your stories, your memories. After all, they're held in the stars themselves, and now that your memory is free, now that he sacrificed his eye, you will see all."

Bannik points to the sky.

I immediately burst into tears.

Soon footsteps sound.

Someone else sits. I think it's the werewolf, Mason. He leans back and points up. "I always favored the fox constellation."

"Bullshit, you favored the pinecone one." Alex's voice reaches us.

Mason sits closest to Bannik and gives him a nod, then

reaches for his hand and squeezes before releasing it.

One by one, the immortals, the council, all lay down and stargaze, and in one final move that has tears streaming down my face, Cassius walks in front of us and waves his hand overhead.

Soft snow begins to fall.

And overhead, the fox constellation starts to run.

Directly into the outstretched arms of the god of the skies.

TWENTY-SEVEN

継続は力なり

Keizoku wa chikara nari

"Continuance is power."

-Japanese proverb

Horus

It's dark.

Dirty.

I'm chained to the wall; I have just enough chains to make it to the edge of the cave and back. I wait for the judgment to come.

Sariel is in the corner sitting upright against the cave wall like it's a vacation in Mexico, and he's taking a siesta, his eyes are closed but he doesn't sleep, nobody can. He gave up everything to get Bannik and me out of this, and now I'm back and joining him.

Apophis is most likely going to have a field day with things she thinks she can take from me. I have the bead, after all. I just hope I can trick her into gaining the tails and leaving with the bead and my life.

No pressure.

"Tough road you've decided to take," Sariel says, eyes still closed. His jet-black hair isn't even messy; it's tied back in a braid that runs down his spine. He's wearing dirty jeans, boots, and a black tank top that already has a rip in it. Blood trickles down his arms.

His wounds are fresh.

Clearly not self-inflicted either.

"I can do this. For her, I can serve this sentence." I repeat this every day, and every day Apophis, my jailer, approaches and asks for the bead.

"Give it over." She holds her hand out. She smells of snake and dirt.

I despise her and keep my eyes trained on the ground.

"Give me the bead, and I'll set you free."

"I want her tails," I counter. "Show me her tails, and we'll talk about the bead."

"The tails are mine!" she screams.

"And the bead is mine." I shrug. "I guess I'll just go take a seat; I'm sure you have more customers, demon goddess."

"I AM THE GODDESS OF THE ABYSS!"

I laugh. "You're the goddess of chaos, and you've lost your way, but if that makes you feel better, by all means, call yourself what you think you are when we all know the truth. You, dear goddess, are so very, very lost."

I sit next to Sariel and think of constellations.

Stars.

I think of Kit, and I draw her constellation in the sand.

TWENTY-EIGHT

相手のない喧嘩はできない

aite no nai kenka wa dekinai

"You can't fight without an opponent."

~Japanese proverb

Kit

They expect me to go back to normal. To just let Bannik work alongside Tarek and me at the bar.

The nightmares are gone.

I can finally sleep like a normal human because I'm slowly becoming exactly that. Even the scars on my back are starting to fade. I'm sure I'll find a gray hair any day now.

I work.

And I work.

And I work some more.

I moved in with Tarek because I wanted to be at the bar, just in case. That's my new mantra, just in case he survives. Just in case he comes back, even though I know that according to Bannik, it could be weeks, years and that while he's down there, it isn't just normal reality.

To the love of my life, the one who went to fix what most could never undo. He's all-powerful, but in chains, he can only sit there and bargain with what he has, and what does he have? One eye left? My bead? What can he possibly sacrifice?

Bannik tells me not to worry, but I can sense his anxiety. It doesn't help that he has the worst temper of any immortal I've ever met in my entire life. God forbid you send back french fries.

We've gotten so many complaints and yet so many compliments on hiring such a handsome staff. Timber's working less since he and Kyra are trying for kids and I do mean aggressively trying, So it's just me, Bannik, and Tarek.

Ugh, the Three Musketeers.

At night, Bannik stays late and asks to watch TV.

Ethan, Alex, Cassius, and Mason stop by constantly to make sure I'm still alive, and it's not because they're worried about my sadness. No, it's because I have a fallen angel sitting on my couch yelling at Simon Cowell to press the golden buzzer, and again, they see his sudden anger, but I think it's because he's also carrying the weight of my sadness on his shoulders. He is my star, after all.

But his inability to stay silent during reality tv is the least of my worries.

Every night, when I go out onto the terrace with a blanket, I find a cup of hot chocolate, a cookie, and a telescope.

Tonight is the same, only this time Bannik's out there. He doesn't need a blanket like I do. He's wearing his uniform, black T-shirt and jeans, but tonight his hair is different.

"You cut it?" I almost reach for it but pull my hand back.

It falls to his shoulders in soft waves of brown and inky red. We've gotten closer in the last three months, almost like siblings that don't talk about all the giant elephants in our shared room.

He shrugs. "We all need change in life." He's clearly uncomfortable. He's not out of a timeline like Horus was, but he feels unworthy to breathe now that Sariel saved him from The Abyss. Now that he has a job and is both mortal and immortal again, he feels like he doesn't deserve.

"Says the guy who wanted to bring the world into chaos." I elbow him trying to get him out of his stupor.

We can at least joke about it now a bit.

He doesn't rage anymore, but he does get sad. I think he needs to talk about it. I know he does, actually. Just like I need to talk about Horus to make sure he still exists.

I watch the stars every night with Bannik, and every night the fox runs to the god.

"Dumb fox," Bannik whispers.

"Dumber god," I say right back as we click our mugs together.

He leans back in his chair, grabbing his own mug of hot chocolate. "Every being is capable of mistakes, but I wonder what makes us deserving." His smile is sad. "I can't hear the songs of the stars anymore. My brothers can, but I was stuck in the Abyss, so I hear... silence."

"What did they say? What did they used to sing?" I ask.

Bannik closes his eyes, and the sound that comes from his mouth is nothing short of heavenly. "Watch. Shine. Breathe. Mine. Ours, the heavenliness wait for you, we wait, oh we wait, dear guardian, blessed by the Creator, we shine down on your face, feel our shine, and when you think of turning away, know you were always meant to stand in that line, to look up, watch us shine." He stops singing. "That was just one verse of thousands."

"They do shine." I reach for his hand. "Very prettily."

"That they do." He squeezes my hand and releases it. "Any news?"

My stomach sinks. "Cassius says he's trying, but we only have silence."

"Silence," Bannik repeats, "is not always the worst. I think I would take silence to noise any day. Noise means chaos, silence means peace." He tilts his head as if thinking, then shrugs. "To some people, I guess."

"Peace," I repeat the word. "I'm going to trust in the peace."

A star shoots across the sky. Slowly, Bannik sets down his hot chocolate and raises both hands to the sky, palms up. "Rest. Rest and shine."

"What just happened?" I ask as Bannik's fingertips glisten with stardust.

He doesn't look at me; he looks up toward the sky and smiles. "A star chose."

"Chose what?"

"To fall." He nods. "As they do. It is always their choice, the journey they want to take, and this one saw theirs."

"How do we know the journey?"

"We don't. We only trust that the end makes it worth it."

I swallow the lump in my throat. "It's that time."

"I know." He sits.

"Tell me." I grab my little purple notebook and open it up, resting my pen against the worn paper. "How many years?"

"As of right now. Horus has been in the Abyss... over a hundred and twenty-seven years, three months, one day, seventeen minutes, four seconds."

I write it down and tuck it close to my heart, then I watch the stars until I fall asleep.

I don't have to ask who brings me to bed; it's always the one that watches me.

It's always Bannik.

What was once a curse became a savior.

A fallen star left by the sky itself.

TWENTY-NINE

四面楚歌

shimensoka

"Surrounded by enemies."

~Japanese proverb

Horus

"Give me the bead!" she screams.

I laugh. "Give me her tails."

"You worthless piece of shit!" Apophis kicks the ground with her feet and stomps off.

Again.

Again.

Again.

"Don't you tire of this?" Sariel asks in a bored tone. I half expect him to yawn. Angels and their dry sense of humor. At least I have him.

"No." I shrug. "What else should I do with my time? I have friends protecting her, and I made a promise to return. I'll bring her tails back, and I'll bring her bead too."

Sariel crosses his arms. "I have to admit, I'm impressed.

In our time, we're now closing in on two hundred years, and you've never wavered."

"Why would I?"

"Do you know my father?" he suddenly asks.

I frown. "Um, the Creator, I think? You are a fallen archangel, after all."

He nods. "Do you ever wonder why a fallen archangel wasn't punished the same as others?"

Now that he mentions it. "I just assumed you were too high up in the heavens."

"Gods." He shrugs. "Sure, the Creator made a race of angels but so did the gods… mine was from the line of Ra. Certain angels have certain jobs, the ones that come from gods watch like the all-seeing Eye of Ra or some might say Horus." He smiles. "The rest of the angels, the warriors, they are from the Creator."

I'm stunned stupid. "How did I not know this?"

"It's not common knowledge. Besides, what would it help? We are all the same species, but some of us have a little extra. The sons of gods were promised that if their immortality ever failed, they would be given one more chance. I took mine in saving my son after my fall, and somehow I ended up here, taking one more chance to save the fallen. I think maybe the Creator thinks I'm even, so I'll try one more time."

"Try what?" I jump to my feet.

Sariel smiles and walks toward the mouth of the cave. "Kings." His whisper is both loud and soft.

Four of the fallen kings of Heaven walk forward. Each of them in chains tied to the very riverbed they're bound to. All of them have black eyes, orange hair and are wearing golden armor that shines so bright it's hard to look at them.

"Angel." Ashtaroth raises his red-tipped sword. "You dare call on us?"

Sariel smiles. "His prison sentence is another hundred and fifty years at least. What if I offer to take it?"

The kings are silent, Mazzaroth, the zodiac fallen angel, steps forward. "We don't allow trades in the Abyss unless the Creator allows it. And he has been absent for centuries."

"And have you called for him?" Sariel asks arms spread.

"We don't dare!" Arcturus says, the man known for being a beast, both angel and demon, both fallen and pure. His skin is that of a bear, his wings tattered at his sides while his bald head shines with gold reflecting the heavens. "We do not call him down to the darkness."

Sariel smiles. "Then would it be fair for darkness and night to call light?"

Ashtaroth frowns. "You dare trick us?"

"He has the bead. He's god of the sky and god of the night. Could he not, just once, call down the Creator? And ask to be set free?"

"We are a void," Ashtaroth says. "Even if his eye burst with the light of a thousand suns, unless a miracle happens, the darkness shades us from the heavens. If he wants to leave this place after coming voluntarily, he must trade."

I nod my head. "Fine. I'll trade."

"What?" Sariel grabs my arm. "What are you saying?"

"Take my other eye; both together are more valuable than one. Just give me the nine tails of the fox and let me leave."

"And the bead?" Ashtaroth asks. "She will want it; she won't let you leave."

"She can have me." A voice sounds. A familiar voice. I pray I'm wrong. It isn't worth this sacrifice. No story should end this way, with pain upon pain and weight on his shoulders, not after being reborn. "I'm sorry, Horus, I promised to watch, and when I did, I saw this. The demon goddess can have me again. Take me, take my power, let him leave with the tails, with the bead, let him have his peace."

"He is a star again!" Ashtaroth says in disbelief. "He was redeemed! He watched her; he watched." He falls to his knees. "His star never chose to fall into The Abyss the first time. But this time... this time, Watcher, Bannik of the Mountain, has chosen to fall. He has chosen. Sacrifice."

Before I can scream no, Bannik is swirled up into darkness yet again. His own hell, the one he just fled, consumes him and tugs him deeper and deeper into the darkness of the Abyss. He doesn't fight it. A tear slides down his cheek. A small smile follows as his body jerks down into the mud; his face is all that's left. "Make it worth my sacrifice, god of the sky, and if you have more power, I wouldn't mind a constellation, even if it is just two stars."

He's tugged through the ground, the mud, and beneath while Sariel yells and is thrust back into the land of the living, able to look up to the stars, while the worst of us is pulled back into the depths of the Euphrates.

Sariel and I hit the riverbed with a thud, and the window to the Abyss closes, sliding down into the running water.

Sariel crumples next to me and looks up. "I'll return, I'll tell the story—"

"Do that." I nod, then grab his hand and point it toward the sky. "And when you speak the words, show them this."

I create a constellation of Bannik.

On his knees.

Sacrificing himself for a fox.

A fallen.

And a god in Hell.

And at the tip of the crown, I place on his head, I create a falling star and point it straight toward Heaven as Sariel is called back home.

THIRTY

雨降って地固まる
ame futte chikatamaru
"When it rains, earth hardens" or "Adversity builds character"
-Japanese proverb

Kit

It's warm in my bed or forest? Where am I? I look around and sit up. Fireflies move around me and my tree. Am I dreaming? Am I back next to where I grew up?

I slowly move to my feet and stumble out into the clearing.

He's there.

It can't be real.

Horus is completely naked, staring up at the sky. "I like it."

"How are you here?"

"Magic." He doesn't turn around. "I heard that when you have a bead and nine tails of a fox, you can basically do anything. Like a dumb god with too much power." His hands are behind his back; slowly, he moves them in front of me and holds them out.

Nine tails.

I count them nine times.

And then I count them again.

Orange, red, blue, pink, white. "How?"

"Everything costs something," he says sadly. "And I had help."

"But, but, this means—"

"Allow me." Horus walks around me and places my tails at my lower back, they press into me and disappear, and suddenly I feel focused again, whole. I don't even miss the bead. I have my tails, the ones cut off, the ones sacrificed. "I don't deserve this."

"You deserve everything." Horus points to the sky. "He does too, but I think his journey is just beginning."

"Who?" I look up and gasp as I see a King of angels. Bannik. His star shoots toward the heavens twisting around and around like a cyclone before bursting across the sky. "He's beautiful."

"He's going to be okay." Horus nods. "Now, about that bead."

"Keep it," I say quickly. "I want you to have a part of me. As long as I have my tails, I can live a long time; I don't need the magic of the bead."

He frowns. "And I do?"

"Yes, god of the sky." I point up. "Because who knows when you'll need to use the power to save a friend?"

"I wouldn't go that far."

"Lie." I laugh. "Now, catch your fox."

I don't run, though. I want to be caught. I also like to

tease. It's been weeks for me, but for him? Hundreds of years.

His kiss is soft, tender.

He lays me down against the grass. "I need you now."

"I need you too."

His lips move down my neck in worship, toward my shoulders, as his hands intertwine with mine. His palms are warm, pressing me back against the ground. My head hits the dirt. The smell of trees and sunshine fills the air. He kicks my legs wide with his own. I welcome him. He releases a hand and rips at my clothing until there's nothing left, then snaps his fingers, he's completely naked.

"Nice trick." I laugh. "Why not use it on me?"

"I wanted to touch you." He grins. "I would never use magic to take away your clothes when I could use my hands and feel you."

Tears fill my eyes. "You're going all romantic on me again."

"I missed you for a very long time." His head descends. "And I'll love you forever, even in the darkness."

He sinks into me, his eyes never leave mine. I'm captivated by the way he stares at me while his hips move. He hasn't even kissed me yet, I'm curious why even as sensations wash over my body.

And then I see it.

Stars shine behind him.

He is, after all, their god.

And I'm now his goddess.

I never want to leave this moment, where the god caught me and kept me for his. Where I caught him and chose him for mine.

Darkness covers us. Stars burn from above as he moves

inside me, his mouth parting, and with each pant, I see flashes of my bead in his eyes. Green, yellow, blue.

Yes, you will see what you worship.

I don't worship my bead.

Or him.

I think what I worship is love.

Us.

He moves hard against me then, shoving me against the soft grass of the forest. "I love you, little fox."

"I love you." I arch beneath him and find my home.

My worship.

In my forest.

EPILOGUE

"Nothing is ever really lost…"
~Sariel, Watcher Proverb

Bannik

She tortures me.
And I smile.
She kicks me, and I embrace the blood.

I've finally found my home in the darkness, not because I've fallen again, but because… I laugh and look up at her. "I am found."

It's what happens when a star chooses and I can't regret that choice. I won't.

I never truly knew the meaning of that word until this moment, watching again. I finally watch.

I watch from the sky.

I suffer from the darkness.

I'm torn between two worlds. I would not choose anything else. I could be on fire one day and given water the next but in all the suffering.

I was able to watch her.

How lovely.

Could an ending ever be this great?

A beginning so tragic?

I nod my head, and I smile again as the fires of The Abyss take hold, but I wait in that moment; I wait for the ice.

And I smile again.

I always thought passion meant a slow burn, but no, the passion I've found, the one I've fought for… it's an icy balm to my soul.

Water in the desert.

Paradise in a dark hell.

I hope they eat their damn ham and laugh.

I hope Horus returned her tails, and she let him keep the bead, the perfect match for the one I watched.

And I hope.

I hope again and again.

And I laugh through the pain of my wings getting cut, blood dripping down. I laugh because I am.

Redeemed.

After all, I am Bannik.

The Watcher.

So even if it is darkness.

I made a promise.

I will watch.

For eternity.

I will finally fulfill my purpose even if all I see is darkness.

EXTENDED EPILOGUE

Horus

"No. I forbid it." I cross my arms. "You're not powerful enough to go out on a girls' date for a day, even two. What if you fall?"

Stephanie curses. "And I thought Cassius was hard on me."

"Hard in—" Alex starts talking; Hope hits him, and he stops. Good choice. "Anyway, the girls are going to go hang out, and then we can go hunt some rogue demons; sounds fun, right?"

He's asking me.

I'm still annoyed.

Doesn't she want to spend every waking moment with me?

"No," Cassius answers like he can read my thoughts. "That's the cause for fights. Let them go, we'll go catch a demon or two." He winces at Timber. "The bad ones."

Timber waves him off. "I like a good run."

"Anyway." Tarek cracks his knuckles. "Are we doing this, or are we doing this?"

Mason pulls up in the Jeep. "Aren't we going?"

Ethan mumbles, "stupid werewolf" at least ten times before stomping over to the car, backtracking, kissing Genesis, then going back to the car.

"He's a true joy when he leaves her. Really, we should make an award or something." Alex shakes his head. "Anyway, let's go!"

Timber and I look at each other, and I realize this is the first time we will actually be together without all the chaos in this timeline, and while we're still working on getting Bannik out and also, you know, helping Sariel out of his stupor, I know things are going to be okay.

They have to be.

We start walking toward the Jeep when a sinister feminine laugh sounds. "Oh, Tarek, you didn't think I forgot about you, did you?"

"NOT IT!" Alex yells. "I'm done with that demon goddess psychopath!"

Tarek grins and rubs his hands together. "Bring it, bitch."

I feel him there. I feel him everywhere.

Sariel.

And at times, Bannik.

I don't know what the Creator has in store for any of us, but I do know that I've been given multiple chances at this life, and she's been given multiple lives for one chance.

Two days after our excursion, I corner her in the apartment above the bar. "Heard there was some bathroom to clean up."

Kit laughs, her shoulders shake, she turns and looks over at me. "What if we use just a little bit of that crazy godlike magic?"

"Fresh out." I lie.

"You're lying."

"Dumb fox."

"Stupid god." She laughs harder. "You have my bead still or at least the essence of it, and I have my tails. You could go down there right now and smite everyone."

"I still refuse to believe that's an actual word."

"You're old; one day, you'll catch up with the dictionary."

I chase her through the apartment. Both of us are in our silly black uniformed shirts, and I don't think I've ever been so happy to tackle her against the couch and tug down her short jean shorts. "I need you."

She bats me away. "We have to work!"

"This is work!" I point out. "It's pleasure and play. I learned this on TikTok."

"Stop following the people in grey sweatpants!" She swats me away. "And just love me the way I'm supposed to be loved—"

"—Got you covered." I tease and tug her jean shorts completely down. "We have around five minutes, right?"

"Huh?" She leans up on her elbows.

My head descends, and I lick, then press a kiss against her right thigh, then her left. "I was always told I was worshipped because I was god of the sky and stars," I smile up at her. "But I think I'd rather make it so that's all you see…" I lick my lips. "The stars."

I don't give her time to think about it.

I choose.

After all, stars, they choose to fall.
My mouth does the same.
I taste.
I embrace.
I create.
And it all starts with her.

AUTHOR NOTE

Surprise! You didn't think I would leave you hanging like that right? We have an entire series to close out and the more I wrote this book the more I was like wow, this started in 2015 and now I still have more story to tell. So yes, of course you get two more books. Tarek and Bannik. They need their happy endings. Tarek releases in the Fall of 2023 and I'm hoping to get Banniks story in maybe around the same time or sooner. I mean, you didn't think that was it right?

WANT MORE RVD?

Did you enjoy Darkest Power?
Then check out the other Supernatural Romances in
THE DARK ONES SAGA!

The Dark Ones Saga
Supernatural Romances — Interconnected Standalones
Dark Origins (Sariel & Nephtal's story)
The Dark Ones (Ethan & Genesis's story)
Untouchable Darkness (Cassius & Stephanie's story)
Dark Surrender (Alex & Hope's story)
Darkest Temptation (Mason & Serenity's story)
Darkest Sinner (Timber & Kyra's story)
Darkest Power (Horus & Kit's story)
Darkest Descent (Bannik's story)
Darkest Desire (Tarek's story)

ACKNOWLEDGMENTS

I'm so thankful to my entire team, to Jill: I swear one day I'll be ahead on things and not stress you out even though you're so gracious, and thank you for all of the late-night plotting and late-night editing! Nina and Nicole, you've been so patient; thank you! Michelle, Krista, Kay, and I know I'm forgetting people but thank you so much guys, for being amazing and helping me finish this.

It was a bit of a struggle only because I had so many ways this could go, and on top of that, I had just written two different pilots for book one, so my mind was completely in TV mode, and I was like, oh wait that has to be on the page oh wait I can do that. It's weird, I know, but it worked out, and I'm so so so happy and thrilled with it!

My husband and two sons, gah, you guys are incredible. I know I get grumpy when I'm on a deadline, so thank you for helping with cooking and shoving chocolate toward me so I can focus!

AND TO MY DAD! FINALLY! You've been asking about this one, and it's always weird writing it because I'm like oh crap, I have to write a sex scene now, but I know you skip those, so it's not weird, lol. We finally did it! I know this book series is your favorite, so please enjoy, and thanks to you and my sister Kristin I got educated and took a deep dive into more history and mythology! So interesting!

As always, and I'm just gonna say this in this acknowledgment, I'm thanking God and my Lord and Savior Jesus Christ for the ability to write books, for being able to wake up and breathe, for the hope I have in knowing that it's never the end—only the beginning. I sometimes see reviews where people have DNF'd my books or stopped reading because it offended them that I mention God in my books, and then I'm always confused until they explain my acknowledgements ruined the book for them. I have to laugh because I'm like, wait people care about what I have to say? They read these? SCORE! GO SEAHAWKS! But also, scroll on through if that triggers you. We all have them, just like we all have our beliefs and convictions, and what an amazing world we live in where we are, for the most part, given the freedom to think and believe what we want.

Again thank you for reading, and yeah, if you're like RVD went all multiverse on us, know that it will all make sense in Bannik's book, but it had to be done this way to make his origin story that spectacular. He's lived lifetimes, he has questions, he has darkness, sadness, and right now, he's suffering for those he loves; he's finally made the ultimate sacrifice.

And he clearly needs a happy ending, as does Tarek.

Thank you for continuing on with these books. As always, you know where to reach me. @RachVD

ABOUT THE AUTHOR

Rachel Van Dyken is the #1 *New York Times*, *Wall Street Journal*, and *USA Today* bestselling author of over 100 books ranging from new adult romance to mafia romance to paranormal & fantasy romance. With over four million copies sold, she's been featured in Forbes, US Weekly, and USA Today. Her books have been translated into more than 15 countries. She was one of the first romance authors to have a Kindle in Motion book through Amazon publishing and continues to strive to be on the cutting edge of the reader experience. She keeps her home in the Pacific Northwest with her husband, adorable sons, a naked cat, and two dogs. For more information about her books and upcoming events, visit www.RachelVanDykenAuthor.com.

ALSO BY RACHEL VAN DYKEN

Eagle Elite
New Adult, Mafia Romance — Interconnected Standalones
Elite (Nixon & Trace's story)
Elect (Nixon & Trace's story)
Entice (Chase & Mil's story)
Elicit (Tex & Mo's story)
Bang Bang (Axel & Amy's story)
Enforce (Elite+ from the boys' POV)
Ember (Phoenix & Bee's story)
Elude (Sergio & Andi's story)
Empire (Sergio & Val's story)
Enrage (Dante & El's story)
Eulogy (Chase & Luciana's story)
Exposed (Dom & Tanit's story)
Envy (Vic & Renee's story)

Elite Bratva Brotherhood
New Adult, Mafia Romance — Interconnected Standalones
RIP (Nikolai & Maya's story)
Debase (Andrei & Alice's story)
Dissolution (Santino & Katya's story)

Mafia Royals Romances
New Adult, Mafia Romance — Interconnected Standalones
Royal Bully (Asher & Claire's story)
Ruthless Princess (Serena & Junior's story)
Scandalous Prince (Breaker & Violet's story)
Destructive King (Asher & Annie's story)
Mafia King (Tank & Kartini's story)
Fallen Royal (Maksim & Izzy's Story)
Broken Crown (King & Del's story)

Rachel Van Dyken & M. Robinson
New Adult, Romantic Suspense — Interconnected Standalones
Mafia Casanova (Romeo & Eden's story)
Falling for the Villain (Juliet Sinacore's story)

The Dark Ones Saga
Supernatural Romances — Interconnected Standalones
Dark Origins (Sariel & Nephtal's story)
The Dark Ones (Ethan & Genesis's story)
Untouchable Darkness (Cassius & Stephanie's story)
Dark Surrender (Alex & Hope's story)
Darkest Temptation (Mason & Serenity's story)
Darkest Sinner (Timber & Kyra's story)
Darkest Power (Horus & Kit's story)
Darkest Descent (Bannik's story)
Darkest Desire (Tarek's story)

Players Game
New Adult, Sports Romances — Interconnected Standalones
Fraternize (Miller, Grant and Emerson's story)
Infraction (Miller & Kinsey's story)
M.V.P. (Jax & Harley's story)

Ruin Series
Upper Young Adult/New Adult, Angsty Romances —
Interconnected Standalones
Ruin (Wes Michels & Kiersten's story)
Toxic (Gabe Hyde & Saylor's story)
Fearless (Wes Michels & Kiersten's story)
Shame (Tristan & Lisa's story)

Seaside Series
Young Adult, Angsty, Rockstar Romances —
Interconnected Standalones
Tear (Alec, Demetri & Natalee's story)
Pull (Demetri & Alyssa's story)
Shatter (Alec & Natalee's story)
Forever (Alec & Natalee's story)
Fall (Jamie Jaymeson & Pricilla's story)
Strung (Tear+ from the boys' POV)
Eternal (Demetri & Alyssa's story)

Seaside Pictures
New Adult, Dramedy (RomCom with Dramatic Moments), Rockstar/Movie Star Romances — Interconnected Standalones
Capture (Lincoln & Dani's story)
Keep (Zane & Fallon's story)
Steal (Will & Angelica's story)
All Stars Fall (Trevor & Penelope's story)
Abandon (Ty & Abigail's story)
Provoke (Braden & Piper's story)
Surrender (Drew & Bronte's story)

Covet
New Adult, Angsty Romances — Interconnected Standalones
Stealing Her (Bridge & Isobel's story)
Finding Him (Julian & Keaton's story)

The Consequence Series
New Adult, Laugh Out Loud Romantic Comedies — Interconnected Standalones
The Consequence of Loving Colton (Colton & Milo's story)
The Consequence of Revenge (Max & Becca's story)
The Consequence of Seduction (Reid & Jordan's story)
The Consequence of Rejection (Jason & Maddy's story)

The Emory Games
New Adult, Laugh Out Loud Romantic Comedies — Standalone Novels
Office Hate (Mark & Olivia's story)
Office Date (Jack & Ivy's story)

Red Card
New Adult, Sports Romances — Interconnected Standalones
Risky Play (Slade & Mackenzie's story)
Kickin' It (Matt & Parker's story)

Standalone Romances
Romantic Comedy, Holiday Romance — Standalone Novel
A Crown for Christmas (Fitz & Phillipa's story)

New Adult, Romantic Comedies — Standalone Novels
Every Girl Does It (Preston & Amanda's story)
Compromising Kessen (Christian & Kessen's story)

New Adult, Fantasy Romance — Standalone Novel
Divine Uprising (Athena & Adonis's story)

Inspirational, Historical Romance — Standalone Novel
The Parting Gift — written with Leah Sanders (Blaine and Mara's story)

Waltzing With The Wallflower — written with Leah Sanders
Regency Romances — Interconnected Standalones
Waltzing with the Wallflower (Ambrose & Cordelia)
Beguiling Bridget (Anthony & Bridget's story)
Taming Wilde (Colin & Gemma's story)

London Fairy Tales
Fairy Tale Inspired Regency Romances —
Interconnected Standalones
Upon a Midnight Dream (Stefan & Rosalind's story)
Whispered Music (Dominique & Isabelle's story)
The Wolf's Pursuit (Hunter & Gwendolyn's story)
When Ash Falls (Ashton & Sofia's story)

Renwick House
Regency Romances — Interconnected Standalones
The Ugly Duckling Debutante (Nicholas & Sara's story)
The Seduction of Sebastian St. James (Sebastian & Emma's story)
The Redemption of Lord Rawlings (Phillip & Abigail's story)
An Unlikely Alliance (Royce & Evelyn's story)
The Devil Duke Takes a Bride (Benedict & Katherine's story)

THE DARK ONES SAGA

www.rachelvandykenauthor.com

Made in the USA
Columbia, SC
03 November 2023

25403667R00159